"Did Daddy tell you not to worry him about domestic matters?"

No matter how hard she tried, Jaz could not hear those words emerging from Connor's mouth.

"Grandma did."

Jaz wondered if she'd go to hell for pumping a child so shamelessly for information. It wasn't for her benefit, she reminded herself. It was for Melanie's. She wanted the child safe and happy. She couldn't even explain why, except she saw her younger self in Melanie.

That and the fact Melanie was Connor's child. The kind of child *she'd* once dreamed of having with Connor.

MICHELLE DOUGLAS

Bachelor Dad
on Her Doorstep

Heart *to* **Heart**

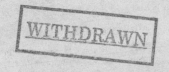

WITHDRAWN

HARLEQUIN®

TORONTO • NEW YORK • LONDON
AMSTERDAM • PARIS • SYDNEY • HAMBURG
STOCKHOLM • ATHENS • TOKYO • MILAN • MADRID
PRAGUE • WARSAW • BUDAPEST • AUCKLAND

Recycling programs
for this product may
not exist in your area.

ISBN-13: 978-0-373-17606-9

BACHELOR DAD ON HER DOORSTEP

First North American Publication 2009.

Copyright © 2009 by Michelle Douglas.

www.eHarlequin.com

Printed in U.S.A.

At the age of eight, **Michelle Douglas** was asked what she wanted to be when she grew up. She answered, "A writer." Years later she read an article about romance writing and thought, *Ooh, that'll be fun.* She was right. When she's not writing she can usually be found with her nose buried in a book. She is currently enrolled in an English master's program for the sole purpose of indulging her reading and writing habits further. She lives in a leafy suburb of Newcastle, on Australia's east coast, with her own romantic hero— —husband Greg, who is the inspiration behind all her happy endings. Michelle would love you to visit her at her Web site, www.michelledouglas.com.

To Varuna, The Writers' House, with thanks.

PROLOGUE

JAZ hadn't meant her first return to Clara Falls in eight years to occur under the cover of darkness, but she hadn't been able to get away from work as early as she'd hoped and then the traffic between Sydney and the Blue Mountains had been horrendous.

She was late.

At least a fortnight too late.

A horrible laugh clawed out of her throat, a sound she'd never heard herself utter before. She tried to drag it back before it swallowed her whole.

Not the time. Not the place.

Definitely not the place.

She didn't drive up Clara Falls' main street. She turned into the lane that led to the residential parking behind the shops. Given the darkness—and the length of time she'd stayed away—would she even recognise the back of the bookshop?

She did. Immediately.

And a weight slammed down so heavily on her chest she sagged. She had to close her eyes and go through the relaxation technique Mac had taught her. The weight didn't lift, but somehow she found a way to breathe through it.

When she could, she opened her eyes and parked her hatchback beside a sleek Honda and stared up at the light burning in the window.

Oh, Mum!

Sorry would not be good enough. It would never be good enough.

Don't think about it.

Not the time. Not the place.

She glanced at the Honda. Was it Richard's car?

Richard—her mother's solicitor.

Richard—Connor Reed's best friend.

The thought came out of nowhere, shooting tension into every muscle, twisting both of her calves into excruciating cramps.

Ha! Not out of nowhere. Whenever she thought of Clara Falls, she thought of Connor Reed. End of story.

She rested her forehead on the steering wheel and welcomed the bite of pain in her legs, but it didn't wipe out the memories from her mind. Connor Reed was the reason she'd left Clara Falls. Connor Reed was the reason she'd never returned.

The cramps didn't ease.

She lifted her gaze back to the bookshop, then higher still to stare at the flat above, where her mother had spent the last two years of her life.

I'm sorry, Mum.

The pain in her chest and legs intensified. Points of light darted at the outer corners of her eyes. She closed them and forced herself to focus on Mac's relaxation technique again— deliberately tensing, then relaxing every muscle in her body, one by one. The pain eased.

She would not see Connor Reed tonight. And, once she'd signed the papers to sell the bookshop to its prospective buyer, she'd never have to set foot in Clara Falls again.

She pushed open the car door and made her way up the back steps. Richard opened the door before she could knock.

'Jaz!' He folded her in a hug. 'It's great to see you.'

He meant it, she could tell. 'I... It's great to see you too.' Strangely enough, she meant it too. A tiny bit of warmth burrowed under her skin.

His smile slipped. 'I just wish it was under different circumstances.'

The warmth shot back out of her. Richard, as her mother's solicitor, had been the one to contact her, to tell her that Frieda had taken an overdose of sleeping pills. To tell her that her mother had died. He hadn't told Jaz that it was all her fault. He hadn't had to.

Don't think about it. Not the time. Not the place.

'Me too,' she managed. She meant *that* with all her heart.

He ushered her inside—into a kitchenette. Jaz knew that this room led through to the stockroom and then into the bookshop proper. Or, at least, it used to.

'Why don't we have a cup of coffee? Gordon should be along any moment and then we can get down to signing all the paperwork.'

'Sure.' She wondered why Richard had asked her to meet him here rather than at his offices. She wondered who this Mr Gordon was who wanted to buy her mother's bookshop.

Asking questions required energy—energy Jaz didn't have.

Richard motioned to the door of the stockroom, 'You want to go take a wander through?'

'No, thank you.'

The last thing she needed was a trip down memory lane. She might've found refuge in this bookshop from the first moment she'd entered it as a ten-year-old. Once upon a time she might've loved it. But she didn't need a refuge now. She was an adult. She'd learned to stand on her own two feet. She'd had to.

'No, thank you,' she repeated.

Her mother had bought the bookshop two years ago in the hope it would lure Jaz back to Clara Falls. She had no desire to see it now, to confront all she'd lost due to her stupid pride and her fear.

Regret crawled across her scalp and down the nape of her neck to settle over her shoulders. She wanted to sell the bookshop. She wanted to leave. *That* was why she was here now.

Richard opened his mouth but, before he could say anything, a knock sounded on the back door. He turned to answer it, ushered a second person into the kitchenette. 'You remember Gordon Sears, don't you, Jaz?'

'Sure I do.'

'It's Mr Sears who wants to buy the bookshop.'

A ball formed in Jaz's stomach. Mr Sears owned the 'baked-fresh-daily' country bakery directly across the road. He hadn't approved of Jaz when she was a child. And he certainly hadn't approved of Frieda.

Mr Sears's eyes widened when they rested on Jaz now, though. It almost made her smile. She sympathised whole-heartedly with his surprise. The last time he'd seen her she'd been a rebellious eighteen-year-old Goth—dressed in top-to-toe black with stark white make-up, spiked hair and a nose ring. Her chocolate-brown woolen trousers and cream knit top would make quite a contrast now.

'How do you do, Mr Sears?' She took a step forward and held out her hand. 'It's nice to see you again.'

He stared at her hand and then his lip curled. 'This is business. It's not a social call.'

He didn't shake her hand.

Memories crashed down on Jaz then. The ball in her stomach hardened, solidified. Mr Sears had never actually refused to serve Jaz and her mother in his 'baked-fresh-daily' country bakery, but he'd let them know by his icy politeness, his curled lip, the placing of change on the counter instead of directly into their hands, what he'd thought of them.

Despite Jaz's pleas, her mother had insisted on shopping there. 'Best bread in town,' she'd say cheerfully.

It had always tasted like sawdust to Jaz.

Frieda Harper's voice sounded through Jaz's mind now. *It doesn't matter what people think. Don't let it bother you.*

Jaz had done her best to follow that advice, but…

Do unto others…

She'd fallen down on that one too.

Frieda Harper, Jaz's wild and wonderful mother. If Frieda had wanted a drink, she'd have a drink. If Frieda had wanted to dance, she'd get up and dance. If Frieda had wanted a man, she'd take a man. It had made the more conservative members of the town tighten their lips in disapproval.

People like Mr Sears. People like Connor Reed's mum and dad.

Jaz wheeled away, blindly groped her way through the all-too-familiar doorways. Light suddenly flooded the darkness, making her blink. She stood in the bookshop…and all her thought processes slammed to a halt.

She turned a slow circle, her eyes wide to take in the enormity of it all. Nothing had changed. Everything was exactly the same as she remembered it.

Nothing had changed.

Oh, Mum…

'I'm sorry, Mr Sears.' It took a moment before she realised it was her voice that broke the silence. 'But it seems I can't sell the bookshop after all.'

'What?'

'Good.'

She heard distinct satisfaction in Richard's voice, but she didn't understand it. She was only aware of the weight lifting from her chest, letting her breathe more freely than she had once during the last two weeks.

CHAPTER ONE

JAZ made the move back to Clara Falls in bright, clear sunlight two weeks later. And this time she had to drive down Clara Falls' main street because an enormous skip blocked the lane leading to the residential parking behind the bookshop.

She slammed on the brakes and stared at it. Unless she turned her car around to flee back to Sydney, she'd have to drive down the main street and find a place to park.

Her mouth went dry.

Turn the car around…?

The temptation stretched through her. Her hands clenched on the steering wheel. She'd sworn never to return. She didn't want to live here. She didn't want to deal with the memories that would pound at her day after day.

And she sure as hell didn't want to see Connor Reed again.

Not that she expected to run into him too often. He'd avoid her the way the righteous spurned the wicked, the way a reformed alcoholic shunned whisky…the way mice baulked at cats.

Good.

Turn the car around…?

She relaxed her hands and pushed her shoulders back. No. Returning to Clara Falls, saving her mother's bookshop—it was the right thing to do. She'd honour her mother's memory; she'd haul the bookshop back from the brink of bankruptcy. She'd do Frieda Harper proud.

Pity you didn't do that a month ago, a year ago, two years ago, when it might have made a difference.

Guilt crawled across her skin. Regret swelled in her stomach until she could taste bile on her tongue. Regret that she hadn't returned when her mother was still alive. Regret that she'd never said all the things she should've said.

Regret that her mother was dead.

Did she honestly think that saving a bookshop and praying for forgiveness would make any difference at all?

Don't think about it! Wrong time. Wrong place.

She backed the car out of the lane and turned in the direction of the main street.

She had to pause at the pedestrian crossing and, as she stared up the length of the main street, her breath caught. Oh, good Lord. She'd forgotten just how pretty this place was.

Clara Falls was one of the main tourist hubs in Australia's breathtaking Blue Mountains. Jaz hadn't forgotten the majesty of Echo Point and The Three Sisters. She hadn't forgotten the grandeur of the Jamison Valley, but Clara Falls…

The artist in her paid silent homage. Maybe she'd taken it for granted all those years ago.

She eased the car up the street and the first stirrings of excitement started replacing her dread. The butcher's shop and mini-mart had both received a facelift. Teddy bears now picnicked in a shop window once crowded with tarot cards and crystals. The wide traffic island down the centre of the road—once grey cement—now sported close-cropped grass, flower-beds and park benches. But the numerous cafés and restaurants still did a bustling trade. This was still the same wide street. Clara Falls was still the same tourist hotspot.

The town had made an art form out of catering to out-of-towners. It had a reputation for quirky arts-and-craft shops, bohemian-style cafés and cosmopolitan restaurants, and… and…darn it, but it was pretty!

A smile tugged at the corners of her mouth. She cruised the

length of the street—she couldn't park directly out the front of the bookshop as a tradesman's van had parked in such a way that it took up two spaces. So, when she reached the end of the street, she turned the car around and cruised back down the other side, gobbling up every familiar landmark along the way.

Finally, she parked the car and sagged back in her seat. She'd spent so long trying to forget Connor Reed that she'd forgotten…stuff she shouldn't have.

Yeah, like how to be a halfway decent human being.

The sunlight abruptly went out of her day. The taste of bile stretched through her mouth again. Her mother had always told Jaz that she needed to return and face her demons, only then could she lay them to rest. Perhaps Frieda had been right— what had happened here in Clara Falls had overshadowed Jaz's entire adult life.

She wanted peace.

Eight years away hadn't given her that.

Not that she deserved it now.

She pushed out of the car. She waited for a break in the traffic, then crossed the road to the island. An elderly man in front of her stumbled up the first step and she grabbed his arm to steady him. She'd crossed at this particular spot more times than she could remember as a child and teenager, almost always heading for the sanctuary of the bookshop. Three steps up, five paces across, and three steps back down the other side. The man muttered his thanks without even looking at her and hurried off.

'Spoilsport,' someone hissed at Jaz. Then to the man, 'And one of these days you'll actually sit down and pass the time of day with me, Boyd Longbottom!'

The elderly woman turned back to Jaz. 'The only entertainment I get these days is watching old Boyd trip up that same step day in, day out.' Dark eyes twinkled. 'Though now you're back in town, Jazmin Harper, I have great hopes that things will liven up around here again.'

'Mrs Lavender!' Jaz grinned. She couldn't help it. Mrs

Lavender had once owned the bookshop. Mrs Lavender had been a friend. 'In as fine form as ever, I see. It's nice to see you.'

Mrs Lavender patted the seat beside her and Jaz sat. She'd expected to feel out of place. She didn't. She nodded towards the bookshop although she couldn't quite bring herself to look at it yet. She had a feeling that its familiarity might break her heart afresh. 'Do you miss it?'

'Every single day. But I'm afraid the old bones aren't what they used to be. Doctor's orders and whatnot. I'm glad you've come back, Jaz.'

This all uttered in a rush. It made Jaz's smile widen. 'Thank you.'

A short pause, then, 'I was sorry about what happened to your mother.'

Jaz's smile evaporated. 'Thank you.'

'I heard you held a memorial service in Sydney.'

'I did.'

'I was sick in hospital at the time or I would have been there.' Jaz shook her head. 'It doesn't matter.'

'Of course it does! Frieda and I were friends.'

Jaz found she could smile again, after a fashion. According to the more uptight members of the town, Frieda might've lacked a certain respectability, but she certainly hadn't lacked friends. The memorial had been well attended.

'This place was never the same after you left.'

Mrs Lavender's voice hauled Jaz back. She gave a short laugh. 'I can believe that.'

Those dark eyes, shrewd with age, surveyed her closely. 'You did the right thing, you know. Leaving.'

No, she hadn't. What she'd done had led directly to her mother's death. She'd left and she'd sworn to never come back. It had broken her mother's heart. She'd hold herself responsible for that till the day she died. And she'd hold Connor responsible too. If he'd believed in Jaz, like he'd always sworn he would, Jaz would never have had to leave.

She would never have had to stay away.

Stop it!

She shook herself. She hadn't returned to Clara Falls for vengeance. Do unto others…that had been Frieda's creed. She would do Frieda Harper proud. She'd save the bookshop, then she'd sell it to someone other than Gordon Sears, then she'd leave, and this time she would never come back.

'You always were a good girl, Jaz. And smart.'

It hadn't been smart to believe Connor's promises.

She shook off the thought and pulled her mind back, to find Mrs Lavender smiling at her broadly. 'How long are you staying?'

'Twelve months.' She'd had to give herself a time limit—it was the only thing that would keep her sane. She figured it'd take a full twelve months to see the bookshop safe again.

'Well, I think it's time you took yourself off and got to work, dear.' Mrs Lavender pointed across the road. 'I think you'll find there's a lot to do.'

Jaz followed the direction of Mrs Lavender's hand, and that was when she saw and understood the reason behind the tradesman's van parked out the front of the bookshop. The muscles in her shoulders, her back, her stomach, all tightened. The minor repairs on the building were supposed to have been finished last week. The receptionist for the building firm Richard had hired had promised faithfully.

A pulse pounded behind her eyes. 'Frieda's Fiction Fair'—the sign on the bookshop's awning—was being replaced. With…

'Jaz's Joint'!

She shot to her feet. Her lip curled. Her nose curled. Inside her boots, even her toes curled. She'd requested that the sign be freshened up. Not… Not… She fought the instinct to bolt across the road and topple the sign-writer and his ladder to the ground.

'I'll be seeing you then, shall I, Jazmin?'

With an effort, she unclenched her teeth. 'Absolutely, Mrs Lavender.'

She forced herself to take three deep breaths, and only then did she step off the kerb of the island. She would sort this out like the adult she was, not the teenager she had been.

She made her way across the road and tried not to notice how firm her offending tradesman's butt looked in form-fitting jeans or how the power of those long, long legs were barely disguised by soft worn denim. In fact, in some places the denim was so worn...

The teenager she'd once been wouldn't have noticed. That girl had only had eyes for Connor. But the woman she was now...

Stop ogling!

She stopped by the ladder and glanced up. Then took an involuntary step backwards at the sudden clench of familiarity. The sign-writer's blond-tipped hair...

It fell in the exact same waves as—

Her heart lodged in her throat, leaving an abyss in her chest. *Get a grip. Don't lose it now.* The familiarity had to be a trick of the light.

Ha! More like a trick of the mind. Planted there by memories she'd done her best to bury.

She swallowed and her heart settled—sort of—in her chest again. 'Excuse me,' she managed to force out of an uncooperative throat, 'but I'd like to know who gave you the authority to change that sign.'

The sign-writer stilled, laid his brush down on the top of the ladder and wiped his hands across that denim-encased butt with agonising slowness. Jaz couldn't help wondering how it would feel to follow that action with her own hands. Gooseflesh broke out on her arms.

Slowly, oh-so-slowly, the sign-writer turned around...and Jaz froze.

'Hello, Jaz.'

The familiarity, the sudden sense of rightness at seeing him here like this, reached right inside her chest to twist her heart until she couldn't breathe.

No!

He took one step down the ladder. 'You're looking…well.'

He didn't smile. His gaze travelled over her face, down the long line of her body and back again and, although half of his face was in shadow, she could see that she left him unmoved.

Connor Reed!

She sucked in a breath, took another involuntary step back. It took every ounce of strength she could marshal to not turn around and run.

Do something. Say something, she ordered.

Her heart pounded in her throat. Sharp breaths stung her lungs. Connor Reed. She'd known they'd run into each other eventually, but not here. Not at the bookshop.

Not on her first day.

Stop staring. Don't you dare run!

'I…um…' She had to clear her throat. She didn't run. 'I'd appreciate it if you'd stop working on that.' She pointed to the sign and, by some freak or miracle or because some deity was smiling down on her, her hand didn't shake. It gave her the confidence to lift her chin and throw her shoulders back again.

He glanced at the sign, then back at her, a frown in his eyes. 'You don't like it?'

'I loathe it. But I'd prefer not to discuss it on the street.'

Oh, dear Lord. She had to set some ground rules. Fast. Ground rule number one was that Connor Reed stay as far away from her as humanly possible.

Ground rule number two—don't look him directly in the eye.

She swung away, meaning to find refuge in the one place in this town she could safely call home…and found the bookshop closed.

The sign on the door read 'Closed' in big black letters. The darkened interior mocked her. She reached out and tested the door. It didn't budge.

Somebody nearby sniggered. 'That's taken the wind out of your sails, nicely. Good!'

Jaz glanced around to find a middle-aged woman glaring at her. She kept her voice cool. 'Excuse me, but do I know you?'

The woman ignored Jaz's words and pushed her face in close. 'We don't need your kind in a nice place like this.'

A disturbance in the air, some super-sense on her personal radar, told her Connor had descended the ladder to stand directly behind her. He still smelt like the mountains in autumn.

She pulled a packet of gum from her pocket and shoved a long spearmint-flavoured stick into her mouth. It immediately overpowered all other scents in her near vicinity.

'My kind?' she enquired as pleasantly as she could.

If these people couldn't get past the memory of her as a teenage Goth with attitude, if they couldn't see that she'd grown up, then…then they needed to open their eyes wider.

Something told her it was their minds that needed opening up and not their eyes.

'A tattoo artist!' the woman spat. 'What do we want with one of those? You're probably a member of a bike gang and… and do drugs!'

Jaz almost laughed at the absurdity. Almost. She lifted her arms, looked down at herself, then back at the other woman. For a moment the other woman looked discomfited.

'That's enough, Dianne.'

That was from Connor. Jaz almost turned around but common sense kicked in—*don't look him directly in the eye*.

'Don't you go letting her get her hooks into you again, Connor. She did what she could to lead you astray when you were teenagers and don't you forget it!'

Jaz snorted. She couldn't help herself. The woman—Dianne—swung back to her. 'You probably think this is going to be a nice little money spinner.' She nodded to the bookshop.

Not at the moment. Not after reviewing the sales figures Richard had sent her.

'You didn't come near your mother for years and now, when

her body is barely cold in the ground, you descend on her shop like a vulture. Like a greedy, grasping—'

'That's enough, Dianne!'

Connor again. Jaz didn't want him fighting her battles—she wanted him to stay as far from her as possible. He wasn't getting a second chance to break her heart. Not in this lifetime! But she could barely breathe, let alone talk.

Didn't come near your mother for years...barely cold in the ground...

The weight pressed down so hard on Jaz's chest that she wanted nothing more than to lie down on the ground and let it crush her.

'You have the gall to say that after the number of weekends Frieda spent in Sydney with Jaz, living the high life? Jaz didn't need to come home and you bloody well know it!'

Home.

Jaz started. She couldn't lie down on the ground. Not out the front of her mother's bookshop.

'Now clear off, Dianne Keith. You're nothing but a trouble-making busybody with a streak of spite in you a mile wide.'

With the loudest intake of breath Jaz had ever heard anyone huff, Dianne stormed off.

Didn't come near your mother for years...barely cold in the ground...

A touch on her arm brought her back. The touch of work-roughened fingers on the bare flesh of her arm.

'Are you okay?'

His voice was low, a cooling autumn breeze. Jaz inched away, out of reach of those work-roughened fingers, away from the heat of his body.

'Yes, I'm fine.'

But, as the spearmint of her gum faded, all she could smell was the mountains in autumn. She remembered how it had once been her favourite smell in the world. When she'd been a girl...and gullible.

She *would* be fine. In just a moment. If she could stop breathing so deeply, his scent would fade.

She cleared her throat. 'It's not that I expected a fatted calf, but I didn't expect that.' She nodded to where Dianne had stood.

She hadn't expected a welcome, but she hadn't expected outright hostility either. Except, perhaps, from Connor Reed.

She'd have welcomed it from him.

'Dianne Keith has been not-so-secretly in love with Gordon Sears for years now.'

She blinked. He was telling her this because… 'Oh! I didn't sell him the bookshop, so his nose is out of joint…making her nose out of joint too?'

'You better believe it.'

She couldn't believe she was standing in Clara Falls' main street talking to Connor Reed like…like nothing had ever happened between them. As if this were a normal, everyday event.

She made the mistake then of glancing full into his face, of meeting his amazing brown eyes head-on.

They sparkled gold. And every exquisite moment she'd ever spent with him came crashing back.

If she could've stepped away she would've, but the bookshop window already pressed hard against her shoulder blades.

If she could've glanced away she would've, but her foolish eyes refused to obey the dictates of her brain. They feasted on his golden beauty as if starved for the sight of him. It made something inside her lift.

The sparks in his eyes flashed and burned. As if he couldn't help it, his gaze lowered and travelled down the length of her body with excruciating slowness. When his gaze returned to hers, his eyes had darkened to a smoky, molten lava that she remembered too well.

Her pulse gave a funny little leap. Blood pounded in her ears. She had to grip her hands together. After all these years and everything that had passed between them, how could there be anything but bitterness?

Her heart burned acid. No way! She had no intention of travelling down that particular path to hell ever again.

Eight years ago she'd believed in him—in them—completely, but Connor had accused her of cheating on him. His lack of faith in her had broken her heart…destroyed her.

She hadn't broken his heart, though, because nine months after Jaz had fled town he'd had a child with Faye. A daughter. A little girl.

She folded her arms. Belatedly, she realised, it made even more of her…assets. She couldn't unfold them again without revealing to him that his continued assessment bothered her. She kept said arms stoically folded, but her heart twisted and turned and ached.

'I don't need you to fight my battles for me, Connor.' She needed him to stay away.

'*I*—' he stressed the word '—always do what I consider is right. You needn't think your coming back to town is going to change that.'

'Do what's right?' She snorted. 'Like jumping to conclusions? Do you still do that, Connor?'

The words shot out of her—a challenge—and she couldn't believe she'd uttered them. The air suddenly grew so thick with their history she wondered how on earth either one of them could breathe through it.

She'd always known things between them could never be normal. Not after the intensity of what they'd shared. It was why she'd stayed away. It was why she needed him to stay away from her now.

'Do what's right?' She snorted a second time. She'd keep up this front if it killed her. 'Like that sign?' She pointed to the shop awning. 'What is that…your idea of a sick joke?'

That frown returned to his eyes again. 'Look, Jaz, I—'

Richard chose that moment to come bustling up between them, his breathing loud and laboured. 'Sorry, Jaz. I saw you cruising up the street, but I couldn't get away immediately. I had a client with me.'

Connor clapped him on the back. 'You need to exercise more, my man, if a sprint up the street makes you breathe this hard.'

Richard grinned. 'It is uphill.'

His grin faded. He hitched his head in the direction of the bookshop. 'Sorry, Jaz. It's a bit of a farce, isn't it?'

'It's not what I was expecting,' she allowed.

Connor and Richard said nothing. She cleared her throat. 'Where are my staff?'

Richard glanced at Connor as if for help. Connor shoved his hands in his pockets and glowered at the pavement.

'Richard?'

'That's just the thing, you see, Jaz. The last of your staff resigned yesterday.'

Resigned? Her staff? So… 'I have no staff?' She stared at Richard. For some reason she turned to stare at Connor too.

Both men nodded.

'But…' She would not lie down on the ground and admit defeat. She wouldn't. 'Why?'

'How about we go inside?' Connor suggested with a glance over his shoulder.

That was when Jaz became aware of the faces pressed against the inside of the plate glass of Mr Sears's 'baked-fresh-daily' country bakery, watching her avidly. In an act of pure bravado, she lifted her hand and sent the shop across the road a cheery wave. Then she turned and stalked through the door Richard had just unlocked.

Connor caught the door before it closed but he didn't step inside. 'I'll get back to work.'

On that sign? 'No, you won't,' she snapped out tartly. 'I want to talk to you.'

Richard stared at her as if…as if…

She reached up to smooth her hair. 'What?'

'Gee, Jaz. You used to dress mean but you always talked sweet.'

'Yeah, well…' She shrugged. 'I found out that I achieved a whole lot more if I did things the other way around.'

Nobody said anything for a moment. Richard rubbed the back of his neck. Connor stared morosely at some point in the middle distance.

'Okay, tell me what happened to my staff.'

'You could probably tell from the sales figures I sent you that the bookshop isn't doing particularly well.'

He could say that again.

'So, over the last few months, your mother let most of the staff go.'

'Most,' she pointed out, 'not all.'

'There was only Anita and Dianne left. Mr Sears poached Anita for the bakery…'

'Which left Dianne.' She swung back to Connor. 'Not the same Dianne who…?'

'The one and the same.'

Oh, that was just great. 'She made her feelings…clear,' she said to Richard.

Richard gave his watch an agonised glance.

'You don't have time for this at the moment, do you?' she said.

'I'm sorry, but I have appointments booked for the next couple of hours and—'

'Then go before you're late.' She shooed him to the door. 'I'll be fine.' She would be.

'I'll be back later,' he promised.

Then he left. Which left her and Connor alone in the dim space of the bookshop.

'So…' Connor said, breaking the silence that had wrapped around them. His voice wasn't so much a cooling autumn breeze as a winter chill. 'You're still not interested in selling the bookshop to Mr Sears?'

Sell? Not in this lifetime.

'I'm not selling the bookshop. At least not yet.'

Connor rested his hands on his hips and continued to survey her. She couldn't read his face or his body language, but she wished he didn't look so darn…male!

'So you're staying here in Clara Falls, then?'

'No.' She poured as much incredulity and disdain into her voice as she could. 'Not long-term. I have a life in the city. This is just a…'

'Just a…' he prompted when she faltered.

'A momentary glitch,' she snapped. 'I'll get the bookshop back on its feet and running at a profit—which I figure will take twelve months tops—and then I mean to return to my real life.'

'I see.'

Perhaps he did. But she doubted it.

CHAPTER TWO

CONNOR met the steeliness in Jaz's eyes and wished he could just turn around and walk away. His overriding instinct was to reach out and offer her comfort. Despite that veneer of toughness she'd cultivated, he knew this return couldn't be easy for her.

Her mother had committed suicide only four weeks ago!

That had to be eating her up alive.

She didn't look as if she'd welcome his comfort. She kept eyeing him as if he were something slimy and wet that had just oozed from the drain.

The muscles in his neck, his jaw, bunched. What was her problem? She'd been the one to lay waste to all his plans, all his dreams, eight years ago. Not the other way around. She could at least have the grace to...

To what? an inner voice mocked. Spare you a smile? Get over yourself, Reed. You don't want her smiles.

But, as he gazed down into her face, noted the fragile luminosity of her skin, the long dark lashes framing her eyes and the sweet peach lipstick staining her lips, something primitive fired his blood. He wanted to haul her into his arms, slant his mouth over hers and taste her, brand himself on her senses.

Every cell in his body tightened and burned at the thought. The intensity of it took him off guard. Had his heart thudding against his ribcage. After eight years...

After eight years he hadn't expected to feel anything. He sure as hell hadn't expected this.

He rolled his shoulders and tried to banish the images from his mind. Every stupid mistake he'd made with his life had happened in the weeks after Jaz had left town. He couldn't blame her for the way he'd reacted to her betrayal—that would be childish—but he would never give her that kind of power over him again.

Never.

She stuck out her chin, hands on hips—combative, aggressive and so unlike the Jaz of old it took him off guard. 'Why did you change the sign? Who gave you permission?'

She moved behind the sales counter, stowed her handbag beneath it, then turned back and raised an eyebrow. 'Well?' She tapped her foot.

Her boot—a pretty little feminine number in brown suede and as unlike her old black Doc Martens as anything could be—echoed smartly against the bare floorboards. Or maybe that was due to the silence that had descended around them again. He hooked his thumbs through the belt loops of his jeans and told himself to stay on task. It was just…that lipstick.

He'd once thought that nothing could look as good as the mulberry dark matt lipstick she'd once worn. He stared at the peach shine on her lips now. He'd been wrong.

'Connor!'

He snapped to and bit back something succinct and rude. *The sign, idiot!*

'I'm simply following the instructions you left with my receptionist.'

She stared at him for a long moment. Then, 'Can you seriously imagine that I'd want to call this place Jaz's Joint?' Her lip curled. 'That sounds like a den of iniquity, not a bookshop.'

She looked vivid fired up like that—alive. It suddenly occurred to him that he hadn't felt alive in a very long time.

He shifted his weight, allowed his gaze to travel over her

again, noticed the way she turned away and bit her lip. *That* was familiar. She wasn't feeling anywhere near as sure of herself as she'd have him believe.

'I'm not paid to imagine.' At the time, though, her request had sent his eyebrows shooting up towards his hairline. 'Eight years is a long time. People change.'

'You better believe it!'

He ignored her vehemence. 'You told my receptionist you wanted "Jaz's Joint" painted on the awning. I was just following your instructions.' But as he said the words his stomach dipped. Her eyes had widened. He remembered how they could look blue or green, depending on the light. They glittered blue now in the hushed light of the bookshop.

'Those weren't my instructions.'

His stomach dropped a notch lower. Not her directions… Then…

'I just requested that the sign be freshened up.'

He swore. Once. Hard.

Jaz blinked. 'I beg your pardon?'

Her tone almost made him grin. As a teenager she'd done all she could to look hard as nails, but she'd rarely used bad language and she hadn't tolerated it in others.

He sobered. 'Obviously, somewhere along the line a wire's got crossed.' If his receptionist had played any part in the *Jaz's Joint* prank he'd fire her on the spot.

Jaz followed his gaze across the road to Mr Sears's bakery. 'Ahh…' Her lips twisted. 'I see.'

Did she? For reasons Connor couldn't fathom, Gordon Sears wanted the bookshop, and he wanted it bad.

She sprang out from behind the counter as if the life force coursing through her body would no longer allow her to coop it up in such a small space. She stalked down the aisles, with their rows upon rows of bookcases. Connor followed.

The Clara Falls bookshop had been designed with one purpose in mind—to charm. And it achieved its aim with remarkable ease. The gleaming oak bookcases contrasted neatly with wood-panelled walls painted a pale clean green. Alcoves and nooks invited browsers to explore. Gingerbread fretwork lent an air of fairy-tale enchantment. Jaz had always loved the bookshop, and Frieda hadn't changed a thing.

Therein lay most of its problems.

'I'll change the sign back. It'll be finished by the close of business today.'

She glanced back at him, a frown in her eyes. 'Why you?'

She turned around fully, folded her arms and leant against the nearest bookcase. To the right of her left hip a book in vivid blues and greens faced outwards—*Natural Wonders of the World*—it seemed apt. He dragged his gaze from her hips and the long, lean length of her legs. Way too apt.

But…

He'd never seen her wear such pretty, soft-looking trousers before. Mel would love those trousers. The thought flitted into his head unbidden and his heart clenched at the thought of his daughter. He gritted his teeth and pushed the thought back out again. He would not think of Mel and Jaz in the same sentence.

But…

Eight years ago he'd grown used to seeing Jaz in long black skirts…or naked.

And then she'd removed herself from his world and he hadn't seen her at all.

'Is that what you're doing these days—sign-writing?'

Her words hauled him back and he steeled himself not to flinch at her incredulity. 'Among other things.' He shoved his hands in his pockets. 'After graduation I took up a carpentry apprenticeship.' He'd relinquished his dream of art school. 'I run a building contractor's business now here in Clara Falls.'

Her jaw dropped. 'What about your art?'

Just for a moment, bitterness seeped out from beneath the lid he normally kept tightly sealed around it. 'I gave it up.'

Her head snapped back. 'You what?'

The madness had started the night he'd discovered Jaz in Sam Hancock's arms. When he'd found out the next day that Jaz had left town—left him—for good, Connor had gone off the rails. He'd drunk too much…he'd slept with Faye. Faye, who'd revealed Jaz's infidelity, her lies. Faye, who'd done all she could to console him when Jaz had gone. Faye whose heart he'd broken. When Faye had told him she was pregnant, he'd had no choice—he'd traded in his dream of art school to become a husband and father…and an apprentice carpenter.

He hadn't picked up a stick of charcoal since.

'Is that somehow supposed to be my fault?'

Jaz's snapped-out words hauled him back. 'Did I say that?'

He and Faye had lasted two years before they'd finally divorced—Jaz always a silent shadow between them. They'd been two of the longest years of his life.

It was childish to blame Jaz for any of that. He had Melanie. He could never regret his daughter.

Jaz's eyes turned so frosty they could freeze a man's soul. Connor's lips twisted. They couldn't touch him. His soul had frozen eight years ago.

And yet she was here. From all accounts a world-class tattoo artist, if Frieda's boasts could be believed.

Dianne was right. Clara Falls had no need for tattoo artists— world-class or otherwise.

And neither did he.

Silence descended around them. Finally, Jaz cleared her throat. 'I take it then that you're the builder Richard hired to do the work on this place?' She lifted a hand to indicate the interior of the shop, and then pointed to the ceiling to indicate the flat upstairs.

'That's right.'

She pushed away from the bookcase, glanced around. 'Considering the amount of work Richard told me needed doing, the place looks exactly as I remember it.'

Her eyes narrowed. He watched her gaze travel over every

fixture and furnishing within her line of sight. '*Exactly* the same.' She turned accusing eyes on him.

'That's because I've barely started work in here yet.'

Her jaw dropped. 'But…but your receptionist assured me all the work would be finished by Thursday last week.'

The muscles in his jaw bunched. 'You're sure about that?'

'Positive.'

He didn't blame her for her gritted teeth response. 'I'm sorry, Jaz, but you were given the wrong information.' And he'd be getting himself a new receptionist— this afternoon, if he could arrange it.

She pressed her lips so tightly together it made his jaw ache in sympathy. Then she stiffened. 'What about the OH and S stuff? Hell, if that hasn't been sorted, then—'

'That's the part I've taken care of.'

Several weeks ago, someone had filed an Occupation Health and Safety complaint. It had resulted in an OH and S officer coming out to inspect the premises…and to close the shop down when it had been discovered that two floor to ceiling bookcases, which should've been screwed fast to battens on the wall behind, had started to come away, threatening to topple and crush anyone who might happen to be below. Connor had put all his other jobs on hold to take care of that. The bookshop had only been closed for a day and a half.

'Why?'

'Why?' What the hell… 'Because it was dangerous, that's why.'

'Not that.' She waved an imperious hand in the air. 'Why is it your company that is doing the work?'

Because Richard had asked him to.

Because he'd wanted to prove that the past had no hold over him any more.

She folded her arms. 'I should imagine the last thing you wanted was to clap eyes on me again.'

She was right about that.

She stuck out a defiant hip. 'In fact, I'd guess that the last thing you want is me living in Clara Falls again.'

It took a moment for the import of her words to hit him. When they did, he clenched a fist so tight it started to shake. She glanced at his fist, then back into his face. She cocked an eyebrow. She didn't unsay her words.

'Are you insinuating that I'd use my position as a builder to sabotage your shop?' He tried to remember the last time he'd wanted to throttle someone.

'Would you? Have you? I mean… There's that travesty of a sign, for a start. Now the delay. What would you think? You and Gordon Sears could be like that—' she waved two crossed fingers under his nose '—for all I know.'

'God, Jaz! I know it's been eight years, but can you seriously think I would stoop to that?'

She raked him from the top of his head to his boot laces with her hot gaze—blue on the way down, green when she met his eyes again on the way up—and it felt as if she actually placed her hands on his body and stroked him. His heart started to thump. She moistened her lips. It wasn't a nervous gesture, more…an assessing one. But it left a shine on her lips that had him clenching back a groan.

'Business is business,' he ground out. 'I don't have to like who I'm working for.'

Was it his imagination or did she pale at his words?

Her chin didn't drop. 'So you're saying this is just another job to you?'

He hesitated a moment too long.

Jaz snorted and pushed past him, charged back down to the sales counter and stood squarely behind it, as if she wanted to place herself out of his reach. 'Thank you for the work you've done so far, Connor, but your services are no longer required.'

He stalked down to the counter, reached across and gripped her chin in his fingers, forced her gaze to his. 'Fine! You want the truth? This isn't just another job. What happened to your mother…

It made me sick to my stomach. We…someone in town…we should've paid more attention, we should've sensed that—'

He released her and swung away. She smelt like a wattle tree in full bloom—sweet and elusive. It was too much.

When he glanced back at her, her eyes had filled with tears. She touched her fingers to her jaw where he'd held her. Bile rose up through him. 'I'm sorry. I shouldn't have—' He gestured futilely with his hand. 'Did I hurt you?'

'No.'

She shook her head, her voice low, and he watched her push the tears down with the sheer force of her will…way down deep inside her like she used to do. Suddenly he felt older than his twenty-six years. He felt a hundred.

'I'm sorry I doubted your integrity.'

She issued her apology with characteristic sincerity and speed. He dragged a hand down his face. The Jaz of old might've been incapable of fidelity, but she'd been equally incapable of malice.

If she'd asked him to forgive her eight years ago, he would have. In an instant.

He shoved his hands in his pockets. 'Am I rehired?'

She straightened, moistened her lips and nodded. He didn't know how he could tell, but this time the gesture was nervous.

'You won't find it hard coping with my presence around the place for the next fortnight?' Some devil prompted him to ask.

'Of course not!'

He could tell that she was lying.

'We're both adults, aren't we? What's in the past is in the past.'

He wanted to agree. He opened his mouth to do precisely that, but the words refused to come.

Jaz glanced at him, moistened her lips again. 'It's going to take a fortnight? So long?'

'Give or take a couple of days. And that's working as fast as I can.'

'I see.'

He shoved his hands deeper into his pockets. 'I'll get back to work on that sign then, shall I?'

The door clanged shut behind Connor with a finality that made Jaz want to burst into tears.

Crazy. Ridiculous.

Her knees shook so badly she thought she might fall. Very carefully, she lowered herself to the stool behind the counter. Being found slumped on the floor was not the look she was aiming for, not on her first day.

Not on any day.

She closed her eyes, dragged in a deep breath and tried to slow her pulse, quieten the blood pounding in her ears. She could do this. She *could* do this. She'd known her first meeting with Connor would be hard. She hadn't expected to deal with him on her first day though.

Hard? Ha! Try gruelling. Exhausting. Fraught.

She hadn't known she would still feel his pain as if it were her own. She hadn't known her body would remember…everything. Or that it would sing and thrum just because he was near.

She hadn't known she'd yearn for it all again—their love, the rightness of being with him.

Connor had shown her the magic of love, but he'd shown her the other side of love too—the blackness, the ugliness…the despair. It had turned her into another kind of person—an angry, destructive person. It had taken her a long time to conquer that darkness. She would never allow herself to become that person again. Never. And the only way she could guarantee that was by keeping Connor at arm's length. Further, if possible.

But it didn't stop her watching him through the shop window as he worked on her sign.

She opened the shop, she served customers, but that didn't stop her noticing how efficiently he worked either, the complete lack of fuss that accompanied his every movement. It reminded her of how he used to draw, of the times they'd take their charcoals and sketch pads to one of the lookouts.

She'd sit on a rock hunched over her pad, intent on capturing every single detail of the view spread out before her, concentrating fiercely on all she saw. Connor would lean back against a tree, his sketch pad propped against one knee, charcoal lightly clasped, eyes half-closed, and his fingers would play across the page with seemingly no effort at all.

Their high school art teacher had given them identical marks, but Jaz had known from the very first that Connor had more talent in his little finger than she possessed in her whole body. She merely drew what was there, copied what was in front of her eyes. Connor's drawings had captured something deeper, something truer. They'd captured an essence, the hidden potential of the thing. Connor had drawn the optimistic future.

His hair glittered gold in the sun as he stepped down the ladder to retrieve something from his van.

And what was he doing now? Painting shop signs? His work should hang in galleries!

He turned and his gaze met hers. Just like that. With no fuss. No hesitation. She didn't step back into the shadows of the shop or drop her gaze and pretend she hadn't been watching. He would know. He pointed to the sign, then sent her a thumbs up.

All that potential wasted.

Jaz couldn't lift her arm in an answering wave. She couldn't even twitch the corners of her mouth upwards in acknowledgement of his silent communication. She had to turn away.

When she'd challenged him—thrown out there in the silences that throbbed between them that she must be the last person he'd ever want to see, he hadn't denied it.

Her stomach burned acid. Coming back to Clara Falls, she'd expected to experience loss and grief. But for her mother. Not Connor. She'd spent the last eight years doing all she could to get over him. These feelings should not be resurfacing now.

If you'd got over him you'd have come home like your mother begged you to.

The accusation rang through her mind. Her hands shook. She hugged herself tightly. She'd refused to come home, still too full of pride and anger and bitterness. It had distorted everything. It had closed her mind to her mother's despair.

If she'd come home…but she hadn't.

For the second time that day, she ground back the tears. She didn't deserve the relief they would bring. She would make a success of the bookshop. She would make this final dream of her mother's a reality. She would leave a lasting memorial of Frieda Harper in Clara Falls. Once she'd done that, perhaps she might find a little peace… Perhaps she'd have earned it.

She glanced back out of the window. Connor hadn't left yet. He stood in a shaft of sunlight, haloed in gold, leaning against his van, talking to Richard. For one glorious moment the years fell away. How many times had she seen Connor and Richard talking like that—at school, on the cricket field, while they'd waited for her outside this very bookshop? Things should've been different. Things should've been very different.

He'd given up his art. It was too high a price to pay. Grief for the boy he'd once been welled up inside her.

It would take her a long, long time to find peace.

She hadn't cheated on him with Sam Hancock. She hadn't cheated on him with anyone, but Connor no longer deserved her bitterness. He had a little daughter now, responsibilities. He'd paid for his mistakes, just like she'd paid for hers. If what her mother had told her was true, Faye had left Connor literally holding the baby six years ago. Jaz would not make his life more difficult.

Something inside her lifted. It eased the tightness in her chest and allowed her to breathe more freely for a moment.

Connor turned and his eyes met hers through the plate glass of the shop window. The weight crashed back down on her with renewed force. She gripped the edges of the stool to keep herself upright. Connor might not deserve her bitterness, but she still had to find a way of making him keep his distance, because something in him still sang to something in her—a siren song that had the power to destroy her all over again if she let it.

Richard turned then too, saw her and waved. She lifted a numb arm in response. He said something to Connor and both men frowned. As one, they pushed away from Connor's van and headed for the bookshop door.

A shiver rippled through her. She shot to her feet. She had to deal with more Connor on her first day? Heaven, give her strength.

The moment he walked through the door all strength seeped from her limbs, leaving them boneless, useless, and plonking her back down on the stool.

'Hello, again,' Richard said.

'Hi.' From somewhere she found a smile.

She glanced sideways at Connor. He pursed his lips and frowned at the ornate pressed-tin work on the ceiling. She found her gaze drawn upwards, searching for signs of damp and peeling paint, searching for what made him frown. She didn't find anything. It all looked fine to her.

Richard cleared his throat and she turned her attention back to him with an apologetic shrug.

'These are the keys for the shop.' He placed a set of keys onto the counter in front of her. 'And this is the key to the flat upstairs.' He held it up for her to see, but he didn't place it on the counter with the other keys.

Connor reached over and plucked the key from Richard's fingers. 'What did my receptionist tell you about the upstairs flat?'

Her stomach started to churn. 'That you'd given it a final coat of paint last week and that it was ready to move into.'

Connor and Richard exchanged glances.

'Um…but then you're a builder, not a painter, right?'

He'd painted the sign for the shop, so maybe…

She shook her head. 'Painting the flat isn't your department, is it?'

'No, but I can organise that for you, if you want.'

'You didn't think to check with me?' Richard asked.

The thought hadn't occurred to her. Though, in hindsight… 'She said she was contacting me on your behalf. I didn't think to question that. When she asked me if there was anything else I needed done, I mentioned the sign.' She'd wanted it bright and sparkling. She wanted her mother's name loud and proud above the shop.

'I'm sorry, Jaz,' Connor started heavily, 'but—'

'But I've been given the wrong information,' she finished for him. Again. From the expression on his face, though, she wouldn't want to be his receptionist when he finally made it back to the office. Shame pierced her. She should've known better than to lump Connor with the meaner elements in the town.

She swallowed. 'That's okay, I can take care of the painting myself.' She wanted to drop her head onto her folded arms and rest for a moment. 'What kind of state is the flat in?'

'We only started tearing out the kitchen cupboards and the rotting floorboards yesterday. It's a mess.'

Once upon a time he'd have couched that more tactfully, but she appreciated his candour now. 'Habitable?'

He grimaced.

'Okay then…' She thought hard for a moment. 'All my stuff is arriving tomorrow.'

'What stuff?' Connor asked.

'Everything. Necessary white goods, for a start—refrigerator, washing machine, microwave. Then there's the furniture—dining table, bed, bookcase. Not to mention the—'

'You brought a bookcase?' Connor glanced around the shop. 'When you have all these?'

For a brief moment his eyes sparkled. Her breathing went all silly. 'I'll need a bookcase in the flat too.'

'Why?'

The teasing glint in his eyes chased her weariness away. 'For the books that happen to be arriving tomorrow too.'

Connor and Richard groaned in unison. 'Has your book addiction lessened as the years have gone by?' Richard demanded.

They used to tease her about this eight years ago. It made her feel younger for a moment, freer. 'Oh, no.' She rubbed her hands together with relish. 'If anything, it's grown.'

The two men groaned again and she laughed. She'd actually laughed on her first day back in Clara Falls? Perhaps miracles could happen.

She glanced at Connor and pulled herself up. Not *those* kinds of miracles.

'Relax, guys. I've rented out my apartment in Sydney. Some of my stuff is to come here, but a lot has gone into storage, including most of my books. Is there room up there to store my things?' She pointed at the ceiling. 'Could you and your men work around it?'

'We'll work quicker if it's stored elsewhere.'

It took her all of two seconds to make the decision. 'Where's the nearest storage facility around here? Katoomba?' She'd organise for her things to go there until the flat was ready.

Connor planted his feet. 'We'll store it at my place.'

She blinked. 'I beg your pardon?'

He stuck his jaw out and folded his arms. 'It's my fault you thought the flat was ready. So it's my responsibility to take care of storing your things.'

'Garbage!' She folded her arms too. 'You had no idea what I was told.' He was as much a victim in this as her. 'I should've had the smarts to double-check it all with Richard anyway.'

'You shouldn't have had to double-check anything and—'

'Guys, guys.' Richard made a time out sign.

Jaz and Connor broke off to glare at each other.

'He does have the room, Jaz. He has a huge workshop with a four car garage for a start.'

She transferred her glare to Richard.

Connor shifted his weight to the balls of his feet. 'This is the last thing you should've had to come back to. You shouldn't be out of pocket because of someone's idea of a…prank.'

It was more than that. They all knew it.

'I'd like to make amends,' he said softly.

She found it hard to hold his gaze and she didn't know why. 'Okay.' She said the word slowly. 'I'll accept your very kind offer—' and it was a kind offer '—on one condition.'

Wariness crept into his eyes. Tiredness invaded every atom of her being. Once upon a time he'd looked at her with absolute trust.

And then he hadn't.

'What's the condition?'

'That you go easy on your receptionist.'

'What?' He leant across the counter as if he hadn't heard her right.

She held his gaze then and she didn't find it hard—not in the slightest. 'She sounded young.'

'She's nineteen. Old enough to know better.'

'Give her a chance to explain.'

He reared back from her then and the tan leached from his face, leaving him pale. Her words had shaken him, she could see that, but she hadn't meant for them to hurt him. From somewhere she dredged up a smile. 'We all make mistakes when we're young. I did. You did.'

'I did,' Richard piped in too.

'Find out why she did it before you storm in and fire her. That's all I'm asking. My arrival has already generated enough hostility as it is.'

Inch by inch, the colour returned to Connor's face. 'If I don't like her explanation, she's still history.'

'But you'll give her an opportunity to explain herself first?'

He glared at her. 'Yes.'

'Thank you.' She couldn't ask for any fairer than that.

They continued to stare at each other. Connor opened his mouth, a strange light in his eyes that she couldn't decipher, and every molecule of her being strained towards him. No words emerged from the firm, lean lips, but for a fraction of a second time stood still.

Richard broke the spell. 'Where were you planning on staying till your stuff arrives, Jaz?'

She dragged her gaze from Connor, tried to still the sudden pounding of her heart. 'I've booked a couple of nights at the Cascade's Rest.'

Richard let the air whistle out between his teeth. 'Nice! Treating yourself?'

'I have a thing for deep spa-baths.' She had a bigger thing for the anonymity that five-star luxury could bring. She couldn't justify staying there for more than a couple of nights, though. 'How long before the flat will be ready?'

'A week to ten days,' Connor said flatly.

She turned back to Richard. 'Is there a bed and breakfast you'd recommend?'

'Gwen Harwood's on Candlebark Street,' he said without hesitation.

Unbidden, a smile broke out from her. 'Gwen?' They'd been friends at school. The five of them—Connor, Richard, Gwen, Faye and herself. They'd all hung out together.

'Look, Jaz.' Connor raked a hand back through the sandy thickness of his hair. 'I can't help feeling responsible for this, and…'

And what? Did he mean to offer her a room too?

Not in this lifetime!

She strove for casual. 'And you have plenty of room, right?' Given all that had passed between them, given all that he thought of her, would he really offer her a room, a bed, a place to stay? The idea disturbed her and anger started to burn low down in the pit of her stomach. If only he hadn't jumped to conclusions eight years ago. If only he'd given her a chance to explain. If only he'd been this nice then!

It's eight years. Let it go.

She wanted to let it go. With all her heart she wished she

could stop feeling like this, but the anger, the pain, had curved their claws into her so fiercely she didn't know how to tear them free without doing more damage.

She needed him to stay away. 'I don't think so!'

The pulse at the base of Connor's jaw worked. 'I wasn't going to offer you a room,' he ground out. 'You'll be happier at Gwen's, believe me. But I will deduct the cost of your accommodation from my final bill.'

Heat invaded her face, her cheeks. She wished she could climb under the counter and stay there. Of course he hadn't meant to offer her a place to stay. Why would he offer her of all people—*her*—a place to stay? Idiot!

'You'll do no such thing!' Pride made her voice tart. 'I had every intention of arriving in Clara Falls today and staying, whether the flat was ready or not.' She'd just have given different instructions to the removal company and found a different place to stay.

No staff. Now no flat. Plummeting profits. What a mess! Where on earth was she supposed to start?

'Jaz?'

She suddenly realised the two men were staring at her in concern. She planted her mask of indifference, of detachment, back to her face in double-quick time. Before either one of them could say anything, she rounded on Connor. 'I want your word of honour that you will bill me as usual, without a discount for my accommodation. Without a discount for anything.'

'But—'

'If you don't I will hire someone else to do the work. Which, obviously, with the delays that would involve, will cost me even more.'

He glared at her. 'Were you this stubborn eight years ago?'

No, she'd been as malleable as a marshmallow.

'Do we have an understanding?'

'Yes,' he ground out, his glare not abating in the slightest.

'Excellent.' She pasted on a smile and made a show of

studying her watch. 'Goodness, is that the time? If you'll excuse me, gentlemen, it's time to close the shop. There's a spa-bath with my name on it waiting for me at the Cascade's Rest.'

As she led them to the door, she refused to glance into Connor's autumn-tinted eyes for even a microsecond.

When Jaz finally made it to the shelter of her room at the Cascade's Rest, she didn't head for the bathroom with its Italian marble, fragrant bath oils and jet-powered spa-bath. She didn't turn on a single light. She shed her clothes, leaving them where they fell, to slide between the cold cotton sheets of the queen-sized bed. She started to shake. 'Mum,' she whispered, 'I miss you.' She rolled to her side, pulled her knees to her chest and wrapped her arms around them. 'Mum, I need you.'

She prayed for the relief of tears, but she'd forced them back too well earlier in the day and they refused to come now. All she could do was press her face to the pillow and count the minutes as the clock ticked the night away.

CHAPTER THREE

JAZ let herself into the bookshop at eight-thirty sharp on Monday morning. She could hear Connor… She cocked her head to one side. She could hear Connor *and* his men hammering away upstairs already.

She locked the front door and headed out the back to the kitchenette. After a moment's hesitation, she cranked open the back door to peer outside. Connor's van—in fact, two vans—had reversed into the residential parking spaces behind the shop, their rear doors propped wide open. Someone clattered down the wooden stairs above and Jaz ducked back inside.

Through the window above the sink, she stared at the sign-writing on the side of the nearest van as she filled the jug—'Clara Falls Carpentry'. A cheery cartoon character wearing a tool belt grinned and waved.

A carpenter. Connor?

Had he painted those signs on the vans?

He was obviously very successful, but did it make up for turning his back on his art, his talent for drawing and painting?

There's nothing wrong with being a carpenter.

Of course not.

And Connor had always been good with his hands. A blush stole through her when she remembered exactly how good.

She jumped when she realised that water overflowed from the now full jug. She turned off the tap and set about making coffee.

Upstairs the banging continued.

Ignore it. Get on with your work.

She had to familiarise herself with the day-to-day running of the bookshop. Managing a small business wasn't new to her—she and her good friend Mac ran their own very exclusive tattoo parlour in Sydney. But she'd been relying on the fact that she'd have staff who could run her through the bookshop's suppliers, explain the accounting and banking procedures… who knew the day-to-day routine of the bookshop.

A mini-office—computer, printer and filing cabinet—had been set up in one corner of the stockroom. The computer looked positively ancient. Biting back a sigh, she switched it on and held her breath. She let it out in a whoosh when the computer booted up. So far, so good.

A glance at her watch told her she had fifteen minutes until she had to open the shop. She slid into the chair, clicked through the files listed on the computer's hard drive and discovered…

Nothing.

Nothing on this old computer seemed to make any sense whatsoever.

She dragged her hands back through her hair and stared at the screen. Maybe all that insomnia was catching up with her. Maybe something here made sense and she just couldn't see it.

Maybe returning to Clara Falls was a seriously bad idea.

'No!' She leapt out of her chair, smoothed down her hair and gulped down her coffee. She'd open the shop, she'd ring the local employment agency…and she'd sort the computer out later.

Without giving herself time for any further negative thoughts, she charged through the shop, unlocked the front door and turned the sign to 'Open'. She flicked through the *Yellow Pages*, found the page she needed, dialled the number and explained to the very efficient-sounding woman at the other end of the line what she needed.

'I'm afraid we don't have too many people on our books at the moment,' the woman explained.

Jaz stared at the receiver in disbelief. 'You have to have more than me,' she said with blunt honesty.

'Yes, well, I'll see what I can do.' The woman took Jaz's details. 'Hopefully we'll have found you something by the end of the week.'

End of the week!

'Uh…thank you,' Jaz managed.

The woman hung up. Jaz kept staring at the receiver. She needed staff now. Today. Not perhaps maybe in a week.

'What's up?'

The words, barked into the silence, made her start. Connor!

She slammed the phone back to its cradle, smoothed down her hair. 'Sorry, I didn't hear the bell above the door.'

The lines of his face were grim, his mouth hard and unsmiling. She fancied she could see him wishing himself away from here. Away from her.

Which was fine. Excellent, actually.

'I asked, what's up?'

No way. She wasn't confiding in him. Not in this lifetime. He wasn't her knight. He wasn't even her friend. He was her builder. End of story.

Derisive laughter sounded through her head. She ignored it. *He was hot.*

She tried to can that thought as soon as she could.

'Nothing's up.'

He wouldn't challenge her. She could tell he wanted out of here asap. Only a friend would challenge her—someone who cared.

'Liar.' He said the word softly. The specks of gold in his eyes sparkled.

She blinked. She swallowed. 'Is this a social call or is there something I can help you with?' The words shot out of her, sounding harder than she'd meant them to.

The golden highlights were abruptly cut off. 'I just wanted to let you know that your things arrived safely yesterday.'

'I…um… Thank you.' She moistened her lips, something

she found herself doing a lot whenever Connor was around. She couldn't help it. She only had to look at him for her mouth to go dry. He started to turn away.

'Connor?'

He turned back, reluctance etched in the line of his shoulders, his neck, his back. Her heart slipped below the level of her belly button. Did he loathe her so much?

She moistened her lips again. His gaze narrowed in on the action and she kicked herself. If he thought she was being deliberately provocative he'd loathe her all the more.

She told herself she didn't care what he thought.

'I'm going to need some of my things. I only brought enough to tide me over for the weekend.' She shrugged, apologetic.

Why on earth should *she* feel apologetic?

His gaze travelled over her. She wore yesterday's trousers and Saturday's blouse. She'd shaken them out and smoothed them the best she could, but it really hadn't helped freshen them up any.

Pride forced her chin up. 'There's just one suitcase I need.' It contained enough of the essentials to get her through. 'I'd be grateful if I could come around this evening and collect it.'

'What's it look like?'

'It's a sturdy red leather number. Big.'

'The one with stickers from all around the world plastered over it?'

'That's the one.' She had no idea how she managed to keep her voice so determinedly cheerful. She waited for him to ask about her travels. They'd meant to travel together after art school—to marry and to travel. They'd planned to paint the world.

He didn't ask. She reminded herself that he'd given all that up. Just like he'd given up on her.

Travel? With his responsibilities?

He'd made his choices.

It didn't stop her heart from aching for him.

She gripped her hands behind her so she wouldn't have to acknowledge their shaking. 'When would it be convenient for me to call around and collect it?'

His eyes gave nothing away. 'Have you booked into Gwen's B&B?'

She nodded.

'Then I'll have it sent around.'

She read the subtext. He didn't need to say the words out loud. It would never be convenient for her to call around. She swallowed. 'Thank you.'

With a nod, he turned and stalked to the door. He reached out, seized the door handle…

'Connor, one final thing…'

He swung back, impatience etched in every line of his body. A different person might've found it funny. 'You and your men are welcome to use the bookshop's kitchenette and bathroom.' She gestured to the back of the shop. The facilities upstairs sounded basic at best at the moment—as in non-existent. 'I'll leave the back door unlocked.'

He strode back and jammed a finger down on the counter between them. 'You'll do no such thing!'

'I beg your pardon?'

'People don't leave their back doors unlocked in Clara Falls any more, Jaz.'

They didn't? She stared back at him and wondered why that felt such a loss.

'And you, I think, have enough trouble without inviting more. Especially of that kind.'

She wanted to tell him she wasn't having any trouble at all, only her mouth refused to form the lie.

'Fine, take the key, then.' She pulled the keys from her pocket and rifled though them. She hadn't worked out what most of them were for yet.

'Here, this one looks a likely candidate.' She held one aloft, sidled out from behind the counter and strode all the way through the shop to the back door again. She fitted the key in the lock. It turned. She wound it off the key ring and shoved it into Connor's hand. 'There.'

'I—'

'Don't let your dislike of me disadvantage your men. They're working hard.'

She refused to meet his gaze, hated the way the golden lights in his eyes were shuttered against her.

'I wasn't going to refuse your offer, Jaz.'

That voice—measured and rhythmic, like a breeze moving through a stand of radiata pine.

'We'll all welcome the chance of a hot drink and the use of that microwave, believe me.'

Amazingly, he smiled. It was a small one admittedly, wiped off his face almost as soon as it appeared, but Jaz's pulse did a little victory dance all the same.

'Do you have a spare? You might need it.'

He held the key between fingers callused by hard work, but Jaz would've recognised those hands anywhere. Once upon a time she'd watched them for hours, had studied them, fascinated by the ease with which they'd moved over his sketch pad. Fascinated by the ease with which they'd moved across her body, evoking a response she'd been powerless to hide.

A response she'd never considered hiding from him.

She gulped. A spare key—he was asking her about a spare key. She rifled through the keys on the key ring. Twice, because she didn't really see them the first time.

'No spare,' she finally said.

'I'll have one cut. I'll get the original back to you by the close of business today.'

'Thank you. Now, I'd better get back to the shop.' But before she left some imp made her add, 'And don't forget to lock the door on your way out. I wouldn't want to invite any trouble, you know.'

She almost swore he chuckled as she left the room.

* * *

At ten-thirty a.m., a busload of tourists descended on the bookshop demanding guidebooks and maps, and depleting her supply of panoramic postcards.

At midday, Jaz raced out to the stockroom to scour the shelves for reserves that would replenish the alarming gaps that were starting to open up in her *Local Information* section. She came away empty-handed.

She walked back to stare at the computer, then shook her head. Later. She'd tackle it later.

At three-thirty a blonde scrap of a thing sidled through the door, barely jangling the bell. She glanced at Jaz with autumn-tinted eyes and Jaz's heart practically fell out of her chest.

Was this Connor's daughter?

It had to be. She had his eyes; she had his hair. She had Faye's heart-shaped face and delicate porcelain skin.

Melanie—such a pretty name. Such a pretty little girl.

An ache grew so big and round in Jaz's chest that it didn't leave room for anything else.

'Hello,' she managed when the little girl continued to stare at her. It wasn't the cheery greeting she'd practised all day, more a hoarse whisper. She was glad Connor wasn't here to hear it.

'Hello,' the little girl returned, edging away towards the children's section.

Jaz let her go, too stunned to ask her if she needed help with anything. Too stunned to ask her if she was looking for her father. Too stunned for anything.

She'd known Connor had a daughter. She'd known she would eventually meet that daughter.

Her hands clenched. She'd known diddly-squat!

Physically, Melanie Reed might be all Connor and Faye, but the slope of her shoulders, the way she hung her head, reminded Jaz of…

Oh, dear Lord. Melanie Reed reminded Jaz of herself at the

same age —friendless, rootless. As a young girl, she'd crept into the bookshop in the exact same fashion Melanie just had.

Her head hurt. Her neck hurt. Pain pounded at her temples. She waited for someone to come in behind Melanie—Connor, his mother perhaps.

Nothing.

She bit her lip. She stared at the door, then glanced towards the children's section. Surely a seven-year-old shouldn't be left unsupervised?

If she craned her neck she could just make out Melanie's blonde curls, could see the way that fair head bent over a book. Something in the child's posture told Jaz she wasn't reading at all, only pretending to.

She glanced at the ceiling. Had Connor asked Melanie to wait for him in here?

She discounted that notion almost immediately. No way.

She glanced back at Melanie. She remembered how she'd felt as a ten-year-old, newly arrived in Clara Falls. She took in the defeated lines of those shoulders and found herself marching towards the children's section. She pretended to tidy the nearby shelves.

'Hello again,' she started brightly. 'I believe I know who you are- -Melanie Reed. Am I right?'

The little face screwed up in suspicion and Jaz wondered if she'd overdone the brightness. Lots of her friends in Sydney had children, but they were all small—babies and toddlers.

Seven was small too, she reminded herself.

'I'm not supposed to talk to strangers.'

Excellent advice, but... 'I'm not really a stranger, you know. I used to live here a long time ago and I knew both your mum and your dad.'

That captured Melanie's interest. 'Were you friends?'

The ache inside her grew. 'Yes.' She made herself smile. 'We were friends.' They'd all been the best of friends once upon a time.

'I can't remember my mum, but I have a picture of her.'

Jaz gulped. According to Frieda, Melanie had only been two years old when Faye had left. 'I…uh…well… It was a long time ago when I knew them. Back before you were born. My name is Jazmin Harper, but everyone calls me Jaz. You can call me Jaz too, if you like.'

'Do you own the bookshop now?'

'I do.'

Melanie gave a tentative smile. 'Everyone calls me Melanie or Mel.' The smile faded. 'I wish they'd call me Melly. I think that sounds nicer, don't you?'

Jaz found herself in total agreement. 'I think Melly is the prettiest name in the world.'

Melanie giggled and Jaz sat herself down on one of the leatherette cubes dotted throughout the bookshop for the relief of foot-weary browsers. 'Now, Melly, I believe your dad is going to be at least another half an hour.'

Melanie immediately shot to her feet, glanced around with wild eyes. 'I'm not supposed to be here. You can't tell him!'

Yikes. 'Why not?'

'Because I'm supposed to go to Mrs Benedict's after school but I hate it there.'

Double yikes. 'Why?'

'Because her breath smells funny…and sometimes she smacks me.'

She smacked her! Jaz's blood instantly went on the boil. 'Have you told your daddy about this?'

Melly shook her head.

'But Melly, why not?'

Melly shook her head again, her bottom lip wobbled. 'Are you going to tell on me?'

Jaz knew she couldn't let this situation go on, but… 'How about I make a deal with you?'

The child's face twisted up in suspicion again. 'What?'

'If you promise to come here after school each afternoon this week, then I won't say anything to anyone.' At least Melly would be safe here.

Melanie's shoulders relaxed. 'Okay.' She shot another small smile at Jaz. 'It's what I always do anyway.'

'There, that's settled then.' Jaz smiled back at her. She figured it would only take her a day or two, till Thursday at the latest, to convince Melanie to confide in Connor.

And she wouldn't like to be in Mrs Benedict's shoes once he found out she'd been smacking his little girl.

'Who picks you up from Mrs Benedict's? Daddy?'

'Yes, at five o'clock on the dot at Mrs Benedict's front gate,' Melly recited.

Jaz glanced at her watch. 'That's nearly an hour away. You know what, Melly? In celebration of making my very first new friend in Clara Falls, I'm going to close the shop early today and walk with you to Mrs Benedict's.'

Melly's eyes grew round. 'I'm your friend?'

'You bet.'

Then Melly beamed at her, really smiled, and the ache pressed so hard against the walls of Jaz's chest that she thought it'd split her open then and there.

Jaz found Connor leaning against the shop front when she arrived at eight-fifteen on Tuesday morning. He held out the key she'd given him yesterday. 'I had a spare one cut. Sorry I didn't get it back to you yesterday.'

She reached out, closed her fingers around it. It still held warmth from his hand. 'Thank you.'

He looked exactly as the radio weatherman had described the weather that morning— cold and clear with a chill in the air, blue skies hinting at the warmth to come later in the day. She didn't know about the warmth to come

'You closed the shop early yesterday.'

No judgement, just an observation. He looked tired.

Something inside her softened to the consistency of water or air…marshmallow.

Not marshmallow! She didn't do marshmallow any more.

But that weariness…it caught at her.

He and Faye had only lasted two years.

Had Connor married Faye on the rebound?

The thought had never occurred to her before. But that marriage… It had happened so fast…

Her knees locked. No! She would not get involved in this man's life again. She would not give him the power to destroy her a second time.

But that weariness…

She hadn't noticed it yesterday or on Saturday. All she'd noticed then was his goldenness. The goldenness might've dimmed, but that didn't make him any less appealing. With his hair damp from a recent shower, the scent of his shampoo enhanced rather than masked the scent of autumn that clung to him.

She tried to pinpoint the individual elements that brought that scent to life, hoping to rob it of its power. A hint of eucalyptus, recently tilled earth…and fresh-cut pumpkin. Those things together shouldn't be alluring. It didn't stop Jaz from wanting to press her face against his neck and gulp in great, greedy breaths.

Good Lord. Stop it!

'I closed fifteen minutes early. I had things to do.'

She wondered if she should tell him about Melanie.

She recalled the way Melly's face had lit up when Jaz had declared them friends and knew she couldn't. Not yet. If Melly hadn't confided in Connor by the end of the week, though, she would have to.

'Have you found new staff yet?' Connor all but growled the words.

Jaz unlocked the door, proud that her hand didn't shake, not even a little. 'I'm working on it.'

'Will someone be in to help today?'

'Perhaps.'

He followed her into the bookshop. 'Perhaps! Do you think that's good enough?'

'I don't think it's any of your concern.'

He followed her all the way through to the kitchenette.

'Coffee?'

Idiot. Mentally she kicked herself. Coffee was way too chummy.

Relief didn't flood her, though, when he shook his head. Work boots thumped overhead and an electric saw rent the air. 'Sorry. I hope we're not disturbing you too much.'

'Not at all.' That didn't bother her in the slightest. Seeing Connor every day…now that was tougher.

Don't go there.

'What time do you start work?' she asked, because it suddenly seemed wise to say something, and fast.

'Seven-thirty.'

She swung around from making coffee. 'Yet you didn't knock off yesterday till just before five?'

One corner of his mouth kinked up as if he'd read the word *slave-driver* in big letters across her forehead. 'My apprentices knocked off at three-thirty.'

But he'd hung around at least an hour longer?

'Look, Connor, you don't need to bust a gut getting the work done in double-quick time, you know. If it takes an extra week or two…' She trailed off with a shrug, hoping she looked as nonchalant as she sounded. He really should be at home spending time with Melly.

His jaw tightened. 'I said it would be completed asap and I meant it. I at least have employees to help me.'

He planted his legs, hands on hips, and Jaz's saliva glands suddenly remembered how to work. Heavens, Connor Reed was still seriously drool-worthy.

'What do you mean to do about it?' he demanded.

She stepped back. Stared. Then she shook herself. He meant her staffing problem.

Of course that was what he meant.

'Get straight to work. That's what I mean to do. I have oodles to get through today.' She wanted to spend between now and nine o'clock trying to coax the secrets out of that ancient computer, particularly the ones that would point her in the direction of her suppliers.

After she'd walked Melly to Mrs Benedict's front gate this afternoon, she'd return and see what else she could coax from it.

Just for a moment, gold sparked from the brown depths of Connor's eyes. 'Have you settled in at Gwen's? Are you comfortable there?'

'Very comfortable, thank you.'

Not true. Oh, her room and en-suite bathroom, the feather bed, were all remarkably comfortable. Gwen's reception, though, hadn't been all Jaz had hoped for.

She made herself smile, saluted Connor with her mug of coffee. 'Now, if you'll excuse me, I have work to do.' Then she fled to the stockroom before those autumn-tinted eyes saw the lies in her own.

The computer did not divulge her suppliers' identities. It didn't divulge much of anything at all. Who on earth was she supposed to phone, fax or email to order in new books? She started clicking indiscriminately on word documents but none of them seemed to hold a clue. Before she had a chance to start rifling through the filing cabinet, it was time to open the shop.

Business wasn't as brisk as it had been the previous day, but she still had a steady stream of customers—all tourists. As she'd had to do the previous day, whenever she went to the bathroom she hung a 'Back in five minutes' sign on the door.

She breathed a sigh when it was time to close the shop and walk Melly the five blocks to Mrs Benedict's front gate.

'Melly, why don't you want to tell your dad that you're unhappy at Mrs Benedict's?'

Melly stopped skipping to survey Jaz soberly. 'Because Daddy has lots of worries and Mrs Benedict is his last hope.' She leaned in close to confide, 'I know because I heard him say so to Grandma. There's no one else who can look after me and I'm too little to stay at home alone.'

'I think your happiness is more important than anything else in the world to your Daddy.' She waited and watched while Melly digested that piece of information. 'Besides,' she added cheerfully, 'there's always me. You're more than welcome to hang out at the bookshop.'

Melly didn't smile. 'Grandad's picking me up today. I stay with him and Grandma on Tuesday nights.'

'That'll be nice.'

Melly didn't say anything for a moment, then, 'Grandma thinks little girls should wear dresses and skirts and not jeans. I don't have any jeans that fit me any more. Yvonne Walker thinks skirts are prissy.'

'Yvonne is in your class at school?' Jaz hazarded.

'She's the prettiest girl in the whole school! And she has the best parties.' Melly's mouth turned down. 'She didn't invite me to her last party.'

Jaz's heart throbbed in sympathy.

'But if she could see my hair like this!'

Melly touched a hand to her hair. Jaz had pulled it up into a ponytail bun. It made Melly look sweet and winsome. 'I'll do it like that for you any time you like,' she promised.

Melly's eyes grew wide.

'And you know what else? I think if you asked your daddy to take you shopping for jeans, he would.'

Jaz waited on the next corner, out of sight, until Melly's grandfather had collected her, then walked back to the shop and installed herself in front of the computer.

She turned it on and stroked the top of the monitor, murmured 'Pretty please,' under her breath.

Above her a set of work boots sounded against bare floorboards, the scrape and squeal of some tool against wood. She glanced up at the ceiling. Why wasn't Connor at home with Melly? Why was he here, working on her flat, when he could be at home with his daughter?

She glanced back at the computer screen and shot forward in her seat when she realised the text on the screen was starting to break up. 'No, no,' she pleaded, placing a hand on either side of the monitor, as if that could help steady it.

Bang! She jumped as a sound like a cap gun rent the air. Smoke belched out of the computer. The screen went black.

'No!'

No staff and now no computer?

She shook the monitor, slapped a fist down hard on top. Nothing.

She sagged in her chair. This couldn't be happening. Not now. *Not now.*

Don't panic.

She leapt to her feet and started to pace. *I won't let you down, Mum.*

The filing cabinet!

With a cry, she dropped to her knees and tried to open the top drawer. Locked. She fumbled in her pockets for the keys. Tried one—didn't fit. Tried a second—wouldn't turn. Tried a third…

The drawer shot open so fast it almost knocked her flat on her back. She rifled through the files avidly. She stopped. She rifled through them again…slowly…and her exultation died. Oh, there were files all right, lots of files. But they were all empty.

She yanked open the second drawer. More files, very neatly arranged, but they didn't contain a damn thing, not even scrap paper. Jaz pulled out each and every one of them anyway, just to check, throwing them with growing ferocity to the floor.

Finally, there were no more to throw. She sat back and stared at the rack and ruin that surrounded her. Maybe Richard had taken the files for safekeeping?

She smoothed down her hair, pulled in a breath and tried to beat back her tiredness.

No, Richard wouldn't have the files. He'd have given them back to her by now if he had.

Maybe her mother hadn't kept any files?

That hardly seemed likely. Frieda Harper had kept meticulous records even for the weekend stall she'd kept at the markets when Jaz was a teenager.

Jaz rested her head on her arm. Which meant Dianne or Anita—or both of them together—had sabotaged the existing files.

'What the bloody hell is going on in here?'

Jaz jumped so high she swore her head almost hit the ceiling. She swung around to find Connor's lean, rangy bulk blocking the doorway to the kitchenette. Her heart rate didn't slow. In fact, her pulse gave a funny little jump.

'Don't sneak up on a person like that!' Hollering helped ease the pulse-jumping. 'You nearly gave me a heart attack!'

'Sorry.' He shoved his hands in his pockets. 'I thought I was making plenty of noise.' His gaze narrowed as it travelled around the room, took in the untidy stack of files on the floor. 'What are you doing?'

'Having a clean out.' She thrust her chin up, practically daring him to contradict her.

For a moment she thought the lines around his mouth softened, but then she realised the light was dim in here and she was tired. She was probably only seeing what she wanted to see.

His nose wrinkled. 'What's that smell?'

'I was burning some incense in here earlier,' she lied.

He stared at her. She resisted the urge to moisten her lips. 'I have a question about a wall,' she said abruptly, gesturing for him to follow her through to the bookshop and away from eau de burning computer.

She was lying through her teeth.

Man, he had to give her ten out of ten for grit.

Keeping one eye on her retreating back, Connor bent to retrieve a file. Empty. Like its counterparts, he guessed, air whistling between his teeth as he flung the file back on the top of the pile.

He glanced at the computer. He knew the smell of a burning motherboard. He'd told Frieda months ago she needed to upgrade that computer. He dragged a hand through his hair, then followed Jaz out into the bookshop.

'This wall here…' She pointed to the wall that divided the kitchenette from the bookshop.

He had to admire her pluck. But that was all he'd admire. He refused to notice the way her hair gleamed rich and dark in the overhead light—the exact same colour as the icing on Gordon Sears's chocolate éclairs. He refused to notice how thick and full it was either or how the style she'd gathered it up into left the back of her neck vulnerable and exposed.

He realised she was staring at him, waiting. He cleared his throat. 'I wouldn't advise building bookshelves on that wall, Jaz.' He rapped his knuckles against it. 'Hear how flimsy it is?'

She stared at him as if she had no idea what he was talking about. 'I can strengthen the wall if you like.' But it'd cost and it'd take time…time she wouldn't want to waste waiting for work to be done if he had her pegged right. 'I could write you up a quote if you want.' What the hell. He'd do the job for cost.

'I don't want bookshelves there. I just want to know if you're doing anything to this wall when you start work down here?'

'No.' One section of floorboards needed replacing and a couple of bookcases needed strengthening, but not the walls.

'So I'm free to paint it?'

'Sure.' He frowned. 'But surely it'd be wiser to wait until all the work is finished, then paint it as a job lot.'

She stared at him. Her eyes were pools of navy a man could drown in if he forgot himself. She moistened her lips—lush, soft lips—and Connor tried not to forget himself.

'I don't mean that kind of painting, Connor.'

It took a moment for her words to make sense. His head snapped back when they did.

She stared at the wall and he knew it wasn't pale green paint she saw.

'I mean to paint a portrait of my mother here.' She turned, a hint of defiance in her eyes, but her whole face had come alive. So alive it made him ache.

A memorial to Frieda? He wanted to applaud her. He wanted to kiss her. He needed his head read. 'Do you mean to start it tonight?'

'No, but I might prime the wall tomorrow.'

For Pete's sake, did she mean to work herself into the ground? 'I thought you'd be back at Gwen's by now.'

'Hmm, no.'

Something in her tone made his eyes narrow. 'Why not?' Jaz and Gwen had been great pals.

She didn't look at him. She cocked her head and continued to survey the wall.

He resisted the urge to shake her. 'Jaz?'

'I think the less Gwen has to see of me, the happier she will be.'

He'd considered Richard's suggestion that Jaz stay at Gwen's an excellent one at the time. He'd thought it'd give Jaz a friend, an ally. He'd obviously got that wrong...and he should've known better. 'Sorry.' The apology dropped stiff from his lips. 'My fault.'

She glanced over her shoulder. 'I hardly think so.'

'I should've thought it through. Gwen...she was pretty cut up when you left. She wouldn't speak to me for months. She kept expecting to hear from you.'

Jaz stiffened, then she swung around, closed the gap between them and gripped his forearms. 'What did you just say?'

Her scent assaulted him and for a moment he found it impossible to speak. Her face had paled, lines of strain fanned out from her eyes. He couldn't remember a time when she'd looked more beautiful. The pressure of her hands on his arms increased, her grip would leave marks, but he welcomed the bite of her nails on his skin.

'She thought you were friends, Jaz. She cared about you.' After him and Faye, Gwen and Richard had been Jaz's closest friends. 'Then you left and she never heard from you again. You can guess how she took that.'

Air hissed out between her teeth. She dropped his arms and stepped back, her eyes wide, stricken—an animal caught in the headlights of an oncoming truck; something wild and injured trying to flee. Without a thought, he reached for her. But she pulled herself up and away, drew in a breath, and he watched, amazed, as she settled a mask of cool composure over her features. As if her distress had never been there at all.

Hell! That couldn't be healthy. He dragged a hand back through his hair, surprised to find that it shook. His heart hammered against his ribcage and he cursed himself for being a hundred different kinds of fool where this woman was concerned.

'Well—' she smiled brightly '—that's me done for the day.' The knuckles on her hands, folded innocuously at her waist, gleamed white. 'So, if you'll excuse me…'

'No!' He cleared his throat, tried to moderate his tone. 'I mean…' Ice prickled across his scalp and the back of his neck. Was it something like this that had tipped Frieda over the edge? 'I mean, where are you going?'

Her eyes had gone wide again. This time with surprise rather than… He didn't know what name to give the expression he'd just witnessed—shock, pain, grief?

'Why, to Gwen's, of course. I have an apology to make.' Sorrow stretched through the navy blue of her eyes. 'I can't believe how shabbily I've treated her. It—'

She waved a hand in front of her face, as if to dispel some image that disturbed her, and he suddenly realised what it was he'd seen in her eyes—self-loathing. She'd never considered herself worthy of his love, or of Faye, Gwen and Richard's friendship, had she?

Why was he only seeing that now?

She glanced at her watch. 'Where's the best place to buy a bottle of wine at this time of night? And chocolate. I'll need chocolate.'

'The tavern's bottle shop will still be open.'

'Thank you.'

She smiled at him and he could see that concern for herself, for the bookshop, had been ousted by her concern for Gwen. He didn't know why that should touch him so deeply. 'Can I give you a lift?'

She snorted. 'Connor, it's a two-minute walk. Thanks all the same, but I'll be fine.'

She stared up at him. He stared back. The silence grew and she moistened her lips. 'I'll see you later then.'

He nodded, dragged in a breath of her scent as she edged past him, then watched as she let herself out of the shop and disappeared into the evening.

He turned to stare at the wall she meant to paint.

With a muffled oath, he strode into the storeroom, disconnected the computer and tucked it under his arm.

He told himself he'd do the same for anyone.

CHAPTER FOUR

AT LUNCHTIME on Wednesday a group of teenagers sauntered through the bookshop's door and it immediately transported Jaz back in time ten years.

Oh, dear Lord. Had she ever looked that…confrontational? She bit back a grin. All of them, boys included, wore tip-to-toe black, the girls in stark white make-up and dark matt lipstick. Between the five of them they had more body piercing than the latest art-house installation on display at the Power House Museum. Their Doc Marten boots clomped heavily against the bare floorboards.

Jaz stopped trying to hold back her grin. She shouldn't smile. They were probably skiving off from afternoon sport at Clara Falls High. But then…Jaz had skived off Wednesday afternoon sport whenever she could get away with it too.

'If there's anything I can help you with, just let me know,' she called out.

'Cool,' said one of the girls.

'Sweet,' said one of the boys.

Jaz went back to studying the book she'd found in the business section half an hour ago—*Everything You Need To Know About Managing a Bookshop*. So far she'd found out that she needed a new computer and an Internet connection.

One of the girls—the one who'd already spoken—seized a book and came up to the counter. 'Every week, I come in here to drool over this book. I can't afford it.'

It was a coffee table art book—*Urban Art.* Exactly the same kind of book Jaz herself had pored over at that age.

'Look, we know the people who used to work here quit.' The girl ran her hands over the cover, longing stretched across her face. 'If I worked here, how many hours would it take me to earn this book?'

Jaz told her.

'Will you hire me? My name is Carmen, by the way. And I'm still at school so I could only work weekends, but... I'll work hard.'

Jaz wanted to reach out and hug her. 'I'm Jaz,' she said instead. They probably knew that already but it seemed churlish not to introduce herself too. 'And yes, I am looking for staff— permanent, part-time and casual.' At the moment she'd take what she could get. 'How old are you, Carmen?'

'Sixteen.'

'I would love to hire you, but before I could do that I would need either your mum or dad's permission.' No way was she going to cause *that* kind of trouble.

Five sets of shoulders slumped. Jaz's grew heavy in sympathy.

'I hate this town,' one of them muttered.

'There's never anything to do!'

'If you look the least bit different you're labelled a trouble-maker.'

Jaz remembered resenting this town at their age too for pretty much the same reasons. 'You're always welcome to come and browse in here.' She motioned to the book on urban art.

'Thanks,' Carmen murmured, but the brightness had left her eyes. She glanced up from placing the book back on its shelf. 'Is it true you're a tattoo artist?'

'Yes, I am.' And she wasn't ashamed of it.

'And are you running drugs through here?'

What? Jaz blinked. 'I could probably rustle you up an aspirin if you needed one, but anything stronger is beyond me, I'm afraid.'

'I told you that was a lie!' Carmen hissed to the others.

'Yeah, well, fat chance that my mum'll let me work here once she catches wind of that rumour,' one of the others grumbled.

The teenagers drifted back outside.

Drugs? Drugs! Jaz started to shake. Her hands curved into claws. Just because she was a tattoo artist that made her a junkie, or a drug baron?

She wished Mac could hear this.

The whole town would boycott her shop if those kinds of rumours took hold. Very carefully, she unclenched her hands. She drummed her fingers against the countertop for a moment, a grim smile touching her lips. Very carefully, she smoothed down her hair. Her smile grew. So did the grimness.

She hooked the 'Back in five minutes' sign to the window, locked the door and set off across the street. 'You'll enjoy this,' she said, without stopping, to Mrs Lavender, who sat on her usual park bench on the traffic island. She reminded herself to walk tall. She reminded herself she was as good as anyone else in this town. Without pausing, she breezed into Mr Sears's shop with her largest smile in place and called out, 'Howdy, Mr Sears! How are you today? Aren't we having the most glorious weather? Good for business, isn't it?'

Mr Sears jerked around from the far end of the shop and his eyes darkened with fury, lines bracketing his mouth, distorting it.

'I'll take a piece of your scrumptious carrot cake to go, thanks.'

The rest of the bakery went deathly quiet. Jaz pretended to peruse the baked goodies on display in their glass-fronted counters until she was level with Mr Sears. 'If you refuse to serve me,' she told him, quietly so no one else heard her, 'I will create the biggest scene Clara Falls has ever seen. And, believe me, you *will* regret it.' Her smile didn't slip an inch.

Mr Sears seized a paper bag. He continued to glare, but he very carefully placed a piece of carrot cake inside it. It was a trait Jaz remembered, and it brought previous visits rushing back. He'd always treated his goods as if they were fine porcelain. For some reason that made her throat thicken.

She swallowed the thickness away. 'Best bread for twenty miles, my mother always used to say,' she continued in her bright, breezy, you're-my-long-lost-best-friend voice. A voice that probably carried all the way outside and across to where Mrs Lavender sat grinning on her park bench.

Carmen emerged from the back of the bakery. 'Hey, Dad, can I…' She stopped dead to stare from her father to Jaz and back again. She swallowed, then offered Jaz a half-hearted smile. 'Hey, Jaz.'

'Hey, Carmen.' Carmen was Gordon Sears's daughter? Whew! His glare grew even more ferocious. She grinned back. *That* was too delicious for words. 'And I'll take a loaf of your famous sourdough too, Mr S.'

He looked as if he'd like to throw the loaf at her head. He didn't. He placed it in a bag and set it down beside her carrot cake. His fingers lingered on the bag, as if in apology to it for where it was going.

Jaz grinned and winked as she paid him. 'It's great to be back in town, Mr S. You have a good day now, you hear?'

He slammed her change on the counter.

'And keep the change.'

She breezed back outside.

To slam smack-bang into Connor. His hands shot out to steady her. His eyes danced with a wicked delight that she feared mirrored her own. 'Lunchtime, huh?'

'That's right. You too?'

'Yep.'

His grin widened. It made her miss…everything.

No, it didn't! She stepped away so he was forced to drop his hands. 'I'd…er…recommend the carrot cake.'

'The carrot cake, huh?'

'That's right.' She swallowed. 'Well… I'll catch ya.' Oh, good Lord. Had she just descended into her former teenage vernacular? With as much nonchalance as she could muster, she stalked off.

His laughter and his hearty, 'Howdy, Mr S,' as he entered the bakery, followed her up the street, across the road and burrowed a path into her stomach to warm her very toes.

She unlocked the bookshop door, plonked herself down on her stool behind the sales counter and devoured her piece of carrot cake. For the first time in her life, Mr Sears's baked goods didn't choke her. The carrot cake didn't taste like sawdust. It tasted divine.

When she closed her eyes to lick the frosting from her fingers all she saw was Connor's laughing autumn eyes, making her feel alive again. In the privacy of the bookshop, she let herself grin back.

An hour after she'd last seen him, Connor stormed into the bookshop with a computer tucked under one arm and the diminutive Mrs Lavender tucked under the other.

Jaz blinked. She tried to slow her heart rate, did what she could to moderate the exhilaration pulsing through her veins. Just because she was back in Clara Falls didn't mean she and Connor were…anything. In fact, it meant the total opposite. They were…nothing. Null and void. History. But…

No man had any right whatsoever to look so darn sexy in jeans and work boots. Thank heavens he wasn't wearing a tool belt. That would draw the eye to…

No, no, no. Jaz tried to shoo that image right out of her head.

Connor set the computer on the counter. Jaz glanced at it, then back at him. She moistened her lips, realised his gaze had narrowed in on that action and her mouth went even drier. 'I know the question is obvious, but…what is that?'

'This is a computer I'm not using at the moment and is yours on loan until you get a chance to upgrade the shop's computer. This—' he pulled a computer disk from his pocket '—is the information my receptionist—the receptionist that I didn't fire and who is a whiz at all things computer—managed to save from your old hard drive. Including several recently deleted files.' He set the disk on top of the computer. 'She's hoping it will go some way to making amends for any previous inconvenience she's caused you.'

Jaz stared at him, speechless.

'And this—' he placed his hands on Mrs Lavender's shoulders '—is Mrs Lavender who, if you remember, owned the bookshop before your mother. A veritable fount of information who is finding herself at a bit of a loose end these days, and who would love to help out for a couple of hours a day, if you're agreeable.'

Agreeable? Jaz wanted to jump over the counter and hug him!

'Gives me a front row seat for watching all the drama. I'll enjoy seeing Gordon Sears brought down a peg or two.' Mrs Lavender's dark eyes twinkled.

Jaz slid out from behind the counter and wrapped her arms around the older woman. Over the top of Mrs Lavender's head, she met Connor's eyes. 'I don't know how to—'

'How's Gwen?'

She straightened and smiled, smoothed down her hair. 'Great.' The word emerged a tad breathy, but Connor was looking at her with such warmth that for a moment she didn't know which way was up.

'Gwen is great.' Gwen had accepted her apology. They'd shared the bottle of wine, they'd eaten the chocolate and they'd forged the beginnings of a new friendship.

He reached out, touched her cheek with the back of one finger. 'Good.' Then he stepped back and shoved his hands into his pockets. 'Time for me to get back to work. I'll see you ladies later.'

He turned, left the shop and disappeared. Only then did Jaz realise he hadn't given her time to thank him. He hadn't given her time to refuse his kindness either. She reached up to touch the spot on her cheek where his finger had lingered for the briefest, loveliest moment.

'Come along, Jaz. We've no time for mooning.'

Mooning? Who was mooning? 'I'm not mooning!'

She gulped. Mrs Lavender was right. She had no time for mooning. Absolutely no time at all.

But that afternoon, before it was time to close the shop and walk Melly home, Jaz's painting supplies were delivered to the bookshop. Connor must've searched through her boxes until he'd found everything she'd need to paint her portrait of Frieda.

She carried the box through to the stockroom, rested her cheek against it for a moment, before setting it to the floor and walking away. It didn't mean anything.

'Have you thought any more about telling your daddy about Mrs Benedict?' Jaz asked Melanie as she walked her to Mrs Benedict's front gate that afternoon.

The child drew herself up as if reciting a lesson. 'I'm not to worry Daddy about domestic matters. He has enough to worry about.'

'Domestic matters?'

'It means household stuff, money and babysitters,' Melly said, rattling each item off as if she'd learned them by heart. 'I checked,' she confided. 'So I'd get it right.'

'Did Daddy tell you not to worry him about domestic matters?' No matter how hard she tried, Jaz could not hear those words emerging from Connor's mouth.

'Grandma did.'

Jaz wondered if she'd go to hell for pumping a child so shamelessly for information. It wasn't for her own benefit, she reminded herself. It was for Melanie's. She wanted the child safe and happy. She couldn't even explain why, except she saw her younger self in Melanie.

That and the fact that Melanie was Connor's child. The kind of child she'd once dreamed of having with Connor.

Which made her sound like some kind of sick stalker! She wasn't. She just wanted to do something...good.

'I think your daddy would be very sad to hear you say that.'

'Why?'

'I think he'd be very interested in everything you do and think, even the domestic ones.'

'Nuh-uh.' The child stuck her chin out and glared at the footpath. 'He was supposed to take me out on the skyway on Saturday, but he didn't coz he had to work.'

Connor had broken a date with his daughter to work on the sign for Jaz's shop!

'Grandma made me promise not to nag him to take me Sunday because she said he'd be tired from working so hard and would need to rest.'

'That was very thoughtful of you.'

Melly glanced up, spearing Jaz with a gaze that touched her to the quick. 'I don't think he needs to work so hard, do you?'

Jaz thought it wiser not to answer that question. 'Perhaps you should tell him you think he's working too hard.'

Melanie shook her head and glanced away. Jaz wondered what else Grandma had made Melanie promise.

'Order, everyone. Order!'

Connor winced. Gordon Sears had a voice that could cut through rock when he was calling a meeting to order. Connor shifted on his seat. Beside him, Richard half-grinned, half-grimaced in sympathy.

'Now, are we all agreed on the winter plantings for the nature strip?'

There were some mutterings, but a show of hands decided the matter. Connor marvelled that it could take so long to decide in favour of hyacinths over daffodils. Personally, he'd have chosen the daffodils, but he didn't much care. It certainly hadn't warranted half an hour's heated debate.

He glanced at his watch. It was almost Mel's bedtime. He hoped his father was coping okay. He tapped his foot against the floor. He didn't like leaving Mel with his parents two nights running. With his mother mostly confined to a wheelchair these days, he considered it too much work for his father. But Russell Reed adored his granddaughter. Mel put a bounce in the older man's step. Connor couldn't deny him that.

When they'd heard Connor was thinking of attending this evening's town meeting, they'd insisted Mel spend the night with them. He bit back a sigh. It was probably for the best. He'd miss reading Mel her bedtime story, but it had started to become all too apparent that Mel hungered for a female influence in her life—a female role model. He'd seen the way she watched the girls at school with their mothers and his heart ached for her.

He was hoping his own mother's presence would help plug that particular hole. At least it gave Mel a woman to confide in. *She needs a younger woman.* He pushed that thought away. Two women had left him without backwards glances. He wasn't going through that again, and he sure as hell wasn't risking his daughter's heart and happiness to some fly-by-night. He and Mel, they'd keep muddling along.

'Now, to the last item on the agenda.'

That rock-cracking voice had Connor wincing again. Richard rolled his eyes at Mr Sears's self-importance. Connor nodded in silent agreement.

'Now, I believe most of you will agree with me when I say we most certainly do not want a tattoo parlour polluting the streets of Clara Falls. Those of you who are in favour of such an abomination, please put forward your arguments now.'

Mr Sears glared around the room. Connor shifted forward on his seat, rested his arms on his knees. This was the reason he'd come tonight.

Nobody put forward an argument for a tattoo parlour in Clara Falls, and Connor listened with growing anger to the plan outlined by Gordon Sears to halt the likelihood of any such development occurring in the future.

Finally, he could stand it no longer. 'I don't know if this has escaped everyone's notice or not,' he said, climbing to his feet, 'but you can't block a non-existent development.'

Mr Sears puffed up. 'That's just semantics!'

'No,' Connor drawled. 'It's law.'

'This town has every right to make its feelings known on the subject.'

Connor planted his feet. 'If you approach Jaz Harper with this viciousness—'

'No names have been mentioned!' Mr Sears bluffed.

'No names have been mentioned, but everyone in this room knows exactly who you're talking about. Jaz Harper has made no move whatsoever to set up a tattoo parlour in Clara Falls. She's come back to run her mother's bookshop. End of story.'

He glanced around the room. Some people nodded their encouragement. Others shifted uneasily on their seats as their gazes slid away. Bloody hell! If Jaz were susceptible to the same kind of depression that had afflicted Frieda then…then she wouldn't need the likes of Gordon Sears banging on her door and shoving a petition under her nose.

'Connor is right.' Richard stood too. 'Last time I checked, this country was still a democracy. If you approach *my client,*' he stressed those two words, 'with a petition or with any other kind of associated viciousness—' he borrowed the term from Connor, but Connor didn't mind '—I will take out a harassment suit on her behalf. And, what's more, I'll enjoy doing it. She's a local businesswoman who is contributing to the economy of this town and we should all be supporting her.'

'I'll second that!' Connor clapped Richard on the back. Richard clapped him back. They both sat down. He watched with grim satisfaction as Gordon Sears brought the meeting to a close in double-quick time.

Mr Sears approached him as he and Richard stood talking by their cars. Connor could sense the anger in the older man, even though he hid it well. 'If any such proposal does go forward to the local council, I want you both to know that I will use every means in my power to block it.'

'I hope you're talking about legal means,' Richard said smoothly.

'Naturally.' Mr Sears lifted his chin and glared at Connor. 'I should've known you'd take her side.'

Connor planted his feet. 'This isn't about sides. It's about keeping Clara Falls as the kind of place where I'm happy to raise my daughter. A place not blinded by small-minded bigotry.'

'Ah, your daughter…yes.'

His smirk made the muscles of Connor's stomach contract.

'I take it that you are aware Melanie has been seen leaving the bookshop with Jaz Harper every afternoon this week?'

She what?

Mr Sears laughed at whatever he saw in Connor's face. 'But, then again, perhaps not.' He strolled off, evidently pleased with the bombshell he'd landed.

'There'll be a perfectly reasonable explanation,' Richard said quietly.

'There'd better be. And I mean to find out what it is.' Now. 'Night, Richard.'

'Night, Connor.'

Connor climbed into his car and turned it in the direction of Frieda's Fiction Fair.

He eased the car past the bookshop at a crawl. A light burned inside, towards the rear of the shop. His lips tightened. She was there. He swung his car left at the roundabout and headed for the parking space behind her shop.

He let himself in with the key Jaz had given him. 'Hello?' He made his voice loud, made sure it'd carry all the way through to the front of the shop. He rattled the door and made plenty of noise. He had no intention of startling her like he had last night.

'Through here,' Jaz called.

He followed the sound of her voice. Then came to a dead halt. She'd started her picture of Frieda.

She was drawing!

He reached out and clamped a hand around the hard shelf of a bookcase as the breath punched out of him. *She looked so familiar.* A thousand different memories pounded at him.

She'd sketched in the top half of Frieda's face with a fine pencil and the detail stole his breath. He inched forward to get a better view. Beneath her fingers, her mother's eyes and brow came alive—so familiar and so...vibrant.

Jaz had honed her skill, her talent, until it sang. The potential he'd recognised in her work eight years ago—the potential anyone who'd seen her work couldn't have failed to recognise—had come of age. An ache started up deep down inside him, settled beneath his ribcage like a stitch.

He wanted to drag his gaze away, but he couldn't.

He found his anger again instead. What the hell was Jaz doing with his little girl? Why had Mel been seen with her every afternoon this week? And why hadn't Mrs Benedict informed him about it?

His hands clenched. He'd protect Mel with every breath in his body. Mel was seven—just a little girl— and vulnerable... And in need of a mother.

He ignored that last thought. Jaz Harper sure as hell didn't fit that bill.

Jaz exhaled, stepped back to survey her work more fully, then she growled. She threw her pencil down on a card table she'd set up nearby—it held a photograph of Frieda—then swung around to him, her eyes blazing. 'I'm grateful for what you did earlier in the day—the loan of the computer, Mrs Lavender et cetera. You left before I could thank you. So...thank you. But you obviously have something on your mind now and you might as well spit it out.'

'I mean to.' He planted his feet, hands on hips. 'I want to know what the hell you've been doing with my daughter every afternoon this week?'

The words shot out of him like nails from a nail gun, startling him with their ferocity, but he refused to moderate his glare. If she'd so much as harmed one hair on Mel's head, he'd make sure she regretted it for the rest of her life.

'Did you hear this from Melanie?'

'Gordon Sears,' he growled.

Jaz's lips twisted at whatever she saw in his face. Lush, full lips. Lips he—

No. He would not fall under her spell again. He wouldn't expose Mel to another woman who'd run at the first hint of trouble.

'Still jumping to conclusions, Connor?'

Her words punched the air out of his body.

'What on earth do you think I've been doing with her?' She planted her hands on her hips—a mirror image of him—and matched his glare. 'What kind of nasty notions have been running through your mind?'

Nothing specific, he realised. But he remembered the gaping hole Jaz had left in his life when she'd fled Clara Falls eight years ago. He wouldn't let her hurt Mel like that.

'One more day,' she whispered. 'That's all I needed with her—one more day.' She said the words almost to herself, as if she'd forgotten he was even there.

'One more day to do what?' he exploded.

She folded her arms, but he saw that her hands shook. 'You haven't changed much at all, have you, Connor? It seems you're still more than willing to believe the worst of me.'

Bile burned his throat.

'I needed one more day to convince her to confide in you, that's what.'

To confide in him… Her words left him floundering. 'To confide what?'

'If you spent a little more time with your daughter, then perhaps you'd know!'

'If I…' His shoulders grew so tight they hurt. 'What do you know about bringing a child up on your own?' About how hard it was. About how the doubts crowded in, making him wonder if he was doing a good job or making a hash of things. About how he'd always be a dad and never a mum and that, no matter how nurturing and gentle he tried to be, he knew it wasn't the same.

'I…nothing.' Jaz took a step back. 'I'm sorry.'

The sadness that stretched across her face had his anger draining away, against his will and against his better judgement. She turned away as if to hide her sadness from him.

'Are you going to tell me what's been going on?' To his relief, his voice had returned to normal.

She started gathering up her pencils and placing them back in their box. 'I don't suppose you'd trust me for just one more day?'

'No, I wouldn't.' He tried to make the words gentle. He had to bite back an oath when she flinched. 'I won't take any risks where Mel's concerned. I can't.'

She smiled then and he saw the same concern she'd shown for Gwen last night reflected in her eyes now. His chest started to burn as if he'd run a marathon. If Jaz had gleaned even the tiniest piece of information that would help him with Mel…Mel, who'd gone from laughing and bright-eyed to sober and withdrawn in what seemed to him a twinkling of an eye.

Mel, who'd once chattered away to him about everything and nothing, and who these days would only shake her head when he asked her if anything was wrong.

'Mel has been coming to the bookshop after school instead of Mrs Benedict's.'

'Do you know why?'

'I…yes, I do.' She hesitated. 'May I ask you a question first?'

His hand clenched. He wanted his bright, bubbly daughter back—the girl whose smile would practically split her face in two whenever she saw him. He'd do anything to achieve that, pay any price. Even if that meant answering Jaz's questions first. He gave a short, hard nod.

'Why is Melly going to Mrs Benedict's after school? Please don't get angry again, but…if you start work at seven-thirty most mornings, surely you should be able to knock off in time to collect Melly from school at three-thirty? Obviously I don't know your personal situation, but it looks as if you're doing well financially. Do you really need to work such long hours?'

No, he didn't.

She frowned. 'And who looks after Melly in the mornings before school?'

'The school provides a care service, before and after school.'

She didn't ask, but he could see the question in her eyes—why didn't he use that service instead of sending Mel to Mrs Benedict's?

'You don't want to tell me, do you?'

What the hell…? That mixture of sadness and understanding in her voice tugged at him. It wouldn't hurt to tell her. It might even go some way to making amends for bursting in here and all but accusing her of hurting Mel.

He raked a hand back through his hair. 'We had a huge storm on this side of the mountain two and a half months ago. It did a lot of damage—roofs blown off, trees down on houses, that kind of thing. The state emergency services were run off their feet and we jumped in to help. We're still getting through that work now. At the time it seemed important to secure people's homes against further damage, to make them safe again…liveable. But it did and does mean working long hours.' He hated to see people homeless, especially families with small children.

'And you feel responsible for making things right?'

He didn't know if that was a statement or a question. He shrugged. 'I just want to do my bit to help.'

'Yes, but don't you think you need to draw the line somewhere? There are more important things in life than work, you know.'

A scowl built up inside him. Did she think work counted two hoots when it came to Mel? Mel was his life.

Jaz thrust her chin out. 'You worked on my sign last Saturday instead of taking Melanie on the skyway. You broke a date with your daughter to work on my stupid sign.'

'You didn't think that sign so unimportant at the time!'

Guilt inched through him. He had cancelled that outing with Mel, but he'd promised to take her to the skyway the next day instead. She'd seemed happy enough with that, as happy as she seemed with anything these days. Except…

He frowned. When Sunday had rolled around Mel had said she didn't want to go anywhere. She'd spent the day colouring in on the living room floor instead.

He should've taken her on the Saturday—he should've kept his promise—but when he'd found out Jaz was expected to arrive in Clara Falls that day, he hadn't been able to stay away. At the time he'd told himself it was to get their initial meeting out of the way, and any associated unpleasantness. As he stared down into Jaz's face now, though, he wondered if he'd lied.

He pulled his mind back. 'It's not just the work. Mel needs a woman in her life. She's —'

He broke off to drag a hand down his face. 'I see the way she watches the girls at school with their mothers.' It broke his heart that he couldn't fill that gap for her. 'She hungers for that…maternal touch.'

Jaz frowned. Then her face suddenly cleared. 'That's what Mrs Benedict's about. She's your maternal touch!'

He nodded. 'She came highly recommended. She's raised five children of her own. She's a big, buxom lady with a booming laugh. A sort of…earth mother figure.'

'I see.'

'I thought that, between her and my mother, they might help fill that need in Mel.'

Scepticism rippled across Jaz's face before she could school it. 'What?' he demanded. From memory, Jaz had never liked his mother.

'Melanie doesn't like going to Mrs Benedict's.'

'She hasn't said anything to me!'

Jaz twisted her hands together again. 'Apparently Mrs Benedict has been smacking her.'

CHAPTER FIVE

'SHE'S what?' Connor reached out and gripped Jaz's shoulders. 'Did you say *smacking her*? Are you telling me Mrs Benedict is *hitting* my daughter?'

'You're hurting me, Connor.'

He released her immediately. And started to pace.

'Relax, Connor, Melly is—'

'Relax? Relax!' How the hell could she say that when—

'Melanie is safe. That's all that matters, right? You can tackle Mrs Benedict tomorrow. Flying off the handle now won't solve anything.'

She had a point. He dragged in a breath. But when he got hold of Mrs Benedict he'd—

'Working out what's best for Melanie is what's important now, isn't it?'

'She's not going back to that woman's place!'

'Good.'

He dragged in another breath. 'So that's why she's been coming here?'

'Yes.'

'And you've been walking her to Mrs Benedict's front gate each afternoon?'

'Yes.'

'And trying to talk her into confiding in me?'

'Yes.'

He ground his teeth together. 'Thank you.'

'It was nothing.'

She tried to shrug his words off, but her eyes were wide and blue. It wasn't nothing and they both knew it.

He unclenched his jaw. 'Do you have any idea why Mel didn't want to confide in me?'

Jaz hesitated again. 'I…'

She did! She knew more about what was going through his daughter's head than he did.

She eyed him warily. 'Will you promise not to shout any more?'

Did she think he'd lash out at her in his anger? He recalled the way he'd stormed in here, and dragged a hand down his face. 'I'll do my best,' he ground out.

'It seems that because you're working so hard, your mother is concerned about your…welfare.'

He frowned. 'I don't get what you're driving at.'

She moistened her lips. He tried to ignore their shine, their fullness…and the hunger that suddenly seized him.

'It seems your mother has been lecturing Melly not to bother you with her troubles when you're so obviously busy with work.'

He gaped at her. No! He snapped his jaw shut. 'You never did like my mother, did you?'

'No, Connor, that's not true, but she never liked me. And in hindsight I can't really blame her. She could hardly have been thrilled that the rebellious Goth girl was going out with her son now, could she?'

His mother had always been…overprotective.

'Look, I'm not making this up.'

He didn't want to believe her…but he did.

She grimaced. 'And, for what it's worth, I think your mother is well-intentioned. She is your mother, after all. It's natural for her to have your best interests at heart.'

'She should have Mel's best interests at heart.' He collapsed onto one of the leatherette cubes. Mel needed a woman in her life, but the two he'd chosen had let her down badly.

And so she'd latched onto Jaz?

What a mess.

This wasn't his mother's fault. It wasn't even Mrs Benedict's fault, though he'd still have some choice words for her when he saw her tomorrow. This was his fault. He hadn't wanted to acknowledge it before and he didn't want to acknowledge it now, but Mel needed a younger woman in her life. Not two women who were at least fifty years older than her.

But Jaz?

'Don't look like that,' Jaz chided. 'This isn't the end of the world. So you knock off from here in time to collect Melly from school for the rest of the week. That's no big deal.'

'It'll put work on the flat back by a day.'

She shrugged again. 'Like I said—no big deal.'

'She didn't confide in me!' The words burst from him, but he couldn't hold them back. Mel had refused to confide in him, but she'd confided in Jaz?

Jaz!

'So you work on winning back her trust. On Saturday you take her out on the skyway. Tell her she looks so pretty you're going to call her Princess Melly for the day and that her every wish is your command.'

He stared at her and he couldn't help it—a grin built up inside him at the image she'd planted in his mind…and at how alive her face had become as she described it. Who called Jaz Princess Jaz? Who tried to make her dreams come true?

He wondered if she'd like to come out on the skyway with him and Mel on Saturday? He wondered if—

Whoa! He pulled back. No way. He was grateful for the insights she'd given him, but not that grateful. Mel might need a younger woman in her life, but Jaz Harper wasn't that woman.

Jaz's smile faltered. 'You want me to butt out now, don't you?'

'Yes.' There was no sense in trying to soften his intentions.

'I see.'

He felt like a heel. He didn't want to hurt her feelings, but he would not—could not—let her hurt Mel. He hardened his heart. 'I don't want you involved in my daughter's life.'

'Good!' Her eyes flashed. 'Because I don't want to be involved in any part of your life either.'

He didn't want what had happened to Frieda happening to Jaz either, though. The thought had him breaking out in a cold sweat. 'I didn't mean that to sound as rotten as it did. It's just…you tell me you're only here for twelve months.'

She folded her arms. 'That's right.'

He swore he glimpsed tears in her eyes. 'Bloody hell, Jaz. If you're only here for twelve months, I don't want Mel getting attached to you. She'll only be hurt when you leave. She won't understand.'

'I hear you, all right!'

Yep, definitely tears. 'Look, I didn't understand when you left eight years ago and I was eighteen. What hope does a seven-year-old have?'

Her jaw dropped and that old anger, the old pain, reared up through him. 'Hell, Jaz! You left and you didn't even tell me why!'

She'd hurt him. Eight years ago, she'd hurt him. She could tell by his pallor, in the way his eyes glittered. In the way the tiredness had invaded the skin around his mouth.

But he'd married Faye so quickly that she'd thought…

She gulped. 'Darn it all, Connor, I was only going to be gone for three months.'

'Three months!' His jaw went slack. His Adam's apple worked. 'Three months?' he repeated before he tensed up again. 'Where the hell did you go? And why didn't you tell me?'

His pain wrapped around her with tentacles that tried to squeeze the air out of her body. She had to drag in a breath before she could speak. 'You have to understand, I was seriously cut up that you thought I could ever cheat on you.'

He hadn't given her a chance to explain at the time. He'd hurled his accusations with all the ferocity of a cornered, injured animal—even then she'd known it was his shock and pain talking, the unexpectedness of finding her at the Hancocks' house, because she had lied about that.

'Stop playing games, Jaz.' He spoke quietly. 'I *know* you were cheating on me with Sam Hancock.'

A spurt of anger rippled through her, followed closely by grim satisfaction. She wanted—no, *needed*—him to keep his distance. If he thought she was the kind of woman who'd cheat on him and still lie about it eight years later, he'd definitely keep his distance.

She was not travelling to hell again with Connor Reed. It had taken too long to get over the last time. He hadn't trusted her then and he didn't trust her now. He'd jumped to conclusions back then and, on this evening's evidence, he still jumped to conclusions now. So much for older and wiser!

'Does it even matter now?' she managed in as frigid a tone as she could muster.

'Not in the slightest. I understand why people cheat. That's not the issue.'

She didn't bother calling him a liar. There didn't seem to be any point. Perhaps it didn't make an ounce of difference to him now anyway.

'What I don't understand is why people run.' He stabbed a finger at her. 'What I don't get is why you left the way you did.'

The flesh on her arms grew cold. If Faye had deserted him too without an explanation…

Was an overdue explanation better than no explanation at all? One glance into his face told her the answer. She pulled in a breath and did what she could to ignore the sudden tiredness that made her limbs heavy. 'Let's just take it as a given that I was in a right state by the time I got home that night, okay?' It made her sick to the stomach just remembering it.

'Fine.' The word emerged clipped and short.

'My mother calmed me down.' Eventually. 'And, bit by bit, got the story out of me.'

'And?' he said when she stopped.

'Did you know that my mother didn't approve of our relationship?'

He blinked and she laughed. Not a mirthful laugh. Definitely not a joyful one. 'I know—funny, isn't it? The rest of the town thought it was me—the rebel Goth girl—leading clean-cut Connor Reed astray.'

'I thought she liked me!'

'She did. But she thought we were too young for such an intense relationship. She was worried I'd put all my dreams on hold for you.'

She could see now that Frieda Harper had had every reason to be concerned. Jaz had been awed by Connor's love—grateful to him for it, unable to believe he could truly love a girl like her. And she'd hidden behind his popularity, his ease with people, instead of standing on her own two feet. Frieda had understood that.

'She asked me to go away from Clara Falls for three months. She begged me to.'

Connor's face had gone white. Jaz swallowed. 'She told me that you and I needed time out from each other, to gain perspective.' And Jaz had been so hurt and so…angry. She'd wanted Connor to pay for the things he'd said. 'She told me that if you really loved me, you'd wait for me.' And Jaz had believed her. 'I went to my aunt's house in Newcastle for three months.' And she'd counted down every single day.

She lifted her head and met his gaze. 'But you didn't wait for me.'

His eyes flashed dark in the pallor of his face. 'Are you trying to put the blame back on me?'

'No.' She shook her head, a black heaviness pressing down on her. 'I'm simply saying you didn't wait.'

He flung an arm in the air. 'I thought you were gone for ever! I didn't think you were ever coming back.'

He'd jumped to conclusions. Again. 'You didn't bother looking for me!'

He took several paces away from her, then swung back. 'Three months?' He stabbed an accusing finger at her. 'You didn't come back!'

The space between them sparked with unspoken resentments and hurts.

Jaz moistened her lips and got her voice back under control. 'The day before I was due to come home, my mother rang. She told me Faye was pregnant and that you were the father. And that you were engaged.'

Connor dragged both hands back through his hair. He collapsed to the leatherette cube as if he'd lost all strength in his legs. Jaz leant heavily against the wall by the unfinished portrait of her mother.

She reached up to touch it, then pulled her hand away at the last moment. She glanced back at Connor. 'You have to see that I couldn't come back once I'd heard that.'

'Why not?'

'There'd be no chance for you and Faye to sort things out if I'd done that.'

She didn't mean to sound arrogant, but it was the truth. For good or ill, she and Connor would've picked straight up where they'd left off—in each other's arms.

He shot to his feet. 'Am I supposed to take that as some kind of noble gesture on your part?'

That tone would've shrivelled her eight years ago. It didn't shrivel her now.

'Noble? Ha!' She glared at him. 'I can't see there's much of anything noble in this entire situation.' She pushed away from the wall. 'But a baby was going to be involved and...and I wasn't going to interfere with that.'

His glare subsided. He bent at the waist, rested his hands on his knees and didn't say anything.

'But how could you?' Her voice shook. 'How could you

sleep with my best friend? Faye, of all people!' The pain of that still ran deep. 'Why Faye?'

Very slowly, he straightened. The emptiness in his eyes shocked her. 'Because she reminded me of you. I was searching for a substitute and she was the nearest I could find.'

The breath left her body. She fell back against the wall. She couldn't think of a single thing to say.

What was there to say? It was all history now. It was too late for her and Connor.

The silence stretched—eloquent of the rift that had grown between them in the intervening years. Connor finally nodded. 'Goodnight, Jaz.' And he made for the door.

For a moment she still couldn't speak. Then, 'If you tell Melly I broke her confidence…it will hurt her.'

He stopped, but he didn't turn around.

'I don't think she deserves that.'

He seemed to think about that and then he nodded. 'You're right.' He took one further step away, stopped again…and then he turned. 'Do you seriously think that, given more time, she would've confided in me?'

'I'm convinced of it.' She tried to find a smile. 'Wait and see. She still might yet.'

She thought he might say something more, but he didn't.

'By the way, did you know that Carmen Sears is looking for an after school job?'

He frowned. 'Why are you telling me this?'

'She'd make a great babysitter for Melanie.'

'But she's—'

He broke off and Jaz couldn't stop her lips from twisting. 'Yes, she's a rebel Goth girl. *And* she seems like a nice kid. Just thought you might be interested, that's all.'

He stared at her for a long moment. 'Why did it take you so long to come back?'

The tone of his voice gave nothing away, and for a brief moment a sense of loss gaped through her. She shrugged and strove for casual. 'Pride, I guess, and resentment at the way things turned out. I was angry with you and Faye. I was angry with my mother. I wanted to forget.'

She shrugged again. She had a feeling she might be overdoing the shrug thing but she couldn't seem to help it. 'In the end it became a habit.' A habit that had broken her mother's heart.

She lifted her chin. 'Goodnight, Connor.'

First thing Thursday morning, Mrs Lavender put Jaz to work changing the book display in the front window. Jaz had a feeling it was a ploy to stop her from fretting about their lack of customers.

'It hasn't been changed in nearly two months. Look, we've all these lovely new bestsellers…and it'll be Mother's Day in a couple of weeks. It needs sprucing up!'

A shaft of pain speared straight into Jaz's heart at the mention of Mother's Day. She kept her chin high, but Mrs Lavender must've seen the strain in her face because she stilled, then reached out and touched Jaz's hand. 'I'm sorry, Jazmin, that was thoughtless of me.'

'Not at all.' She gulped. She would not let her chin drop. 'I'm the one who didn't come back for the past eight Mother's Days. I have no right to self-pity now.' Oh, she'd sent flowers, had phoned, but it wasn't the same.

'You have a right to your grief.'

Jaz managed a weak smile, but she didn't answer. She deserved to spend this coming Mother's Day burning with guilt.

She made Mrs Lavender a cup of tea, noticed Connor's truck parked out the back, and the burning in her chest increased ten-fold.

'Have you looked these over, Jaz?'

Jaz had just climbed out of the window, pleased with her brand new display. She glanced over Mrs Lavender's shoulder. 'Oh, those.' A printout of the sales figures for the last three months. A weight dropped to her shoulders and crashed and banged and did what it could to hammer her through the floor. 'Appalling, aren't they?'

'You have to turn these around, and fast.' There was no mistaking Mrs Lavender's concern. 'Jaz, this is serious.'

'I…' She was doing all she could.

Mrs Lavender tapped her pen against the counter, ummed and ahhed under her breath. Then her face suddenly lit up. 'We'll have a book fair, that's what we'll do! It'll stir up some interest in this place again.'

'A book fair?'

'We'll get in entertainment for the kiddies, we'll have readings by local authors… We'll have a ten per cent sale on all our books. We'll get people excited. We'll get people to come. And, by golly, we'll save this bookshop!'

Jaz clutched her hands together. 'Do you think it could work?'

'My dear Jazmin, we're going to have to make it work. Either that or make the decision to sell up to Mr Sears.'

'No!' She cast a glance towards the back wall and the unfinished portrait of Frieda. 'I'm not selling to him.' She hitched up her chin. 'We'll have a book fair.'

She and Mrs Lavender spent the rest of the morning planning a full-page advertisement in the local newspaper. They discussed children's entertainment. Jaz started to design posters and flyers. They settled on the day—the Saturday of the Mother's Day weekend.

If the book fair didn't work…

Jaz shook her head. She refused to think about that.

At midday Mrs Lavender excused herself to go and sit on her usual park bench to torment Boyd Longbottom.

'What's the story with you and Boyd Longbottom, anyway?' Jaz asked.

'He was a beau of mine, a long time ago.'

Jaz set her pen down. 'Really?'

'But when I chose my Arthur over him, he swore he'd never speak to me again. He's kept his word to this very day.'

'But that's awful.'

'He never left Clara Falls. He never married. And he's not spoken to me again, not once.'

'That's…sad.'

'Yes, Jaz, it is.' Mrs Lavender opened her mouth as if she meant to say more, but she shut it again. 'I'll see you tomorrow.'

At quarter past twelve Connor jogged across the street to Mr Sears's bakery. On his way back he stopped right outside the bookshop window to survey the new display.

Jaz stood behind one of the bookcases she was tidying and watched him. Her heart squeezed so tight the blood rushed in her ears.

Turn your back. Walk away.

Her body refused to obey the dictates of her brain.

At least close your eyes.

She didn't obey that order either. She remembered how she and Connor had once shared their drawings with each other, offering praise or criticism, suggestions for improvements. She searched his face. Did he like her display?

She couldn't tell.

He didn't lift his eyes and search for her inside the shop.

Eventually he turned and strode away. The tightness around Jaz's heart eased, but nothing could expand to fill the gap that yawned through her.

At a touch after three-thirty the phone rang. Jaz pounced on it, eager to take her mind off the fact that Melly wasn't here. She'd known Melly wouldn't show up here today. Just as she knew Melly wouldn't show up here tomorrow…or any other day from now on.

She didn't know why it should make her feel lonely, only that it did.

'Hey, mate!' Her business partner's voice boomed down the line at her. 'How're you doing?'

'Mac!' She grinned. 'Better now that I'm talking to you. How are Bonnie and the kids?'

'They send their love. Now, tell me, has the town welcomed you back with open arms?'

'Yes and no. Business could be a lot better, though. I'm not getting any local trade.'

'Are they giving you a hard time?'

'Well, there is a rumour that I'm the local drug baron.'

His laughter roared down the line, lifting her spirits. 'What? Little Ms Clean-as-a-Whistle Jaz Harper?' He sobered. 'I bet that's doing wonders for business.'

'Ooh, yeah.'

'Listen, mate, I have a job for you, and I have a plan.'

Her smile widened as she listened to his plan.

CHAPTER SIX

'OKAY, Princess Melly—' Connor held the door to Mr Sears's bakery open '—what is your pleasure?'

Mel's eyes danced. It gladdened Connor's heart.

'Princess Melly wants a picnic!'

'Where…at the park? Or perhaps at one of the lookouts?' He cocked his head to one side. 'On the skyway?' They'd already been back and across on the skyway twice this morning.

Over the course of the morning Mel had laughed with her whole self, and it made things inside him grateful and light. She'd retreated into her shell a couple of times, but so far she'd come peeping back out again.

Jaz had been right. The Princess Melly thing was working a treat. It had disarmed his daughter almost immediately—that and the skyway rides. Not to mention the jeans-buying expedition. Mel had only requested one pair of jeans, but it had suddenly occurred to Connor that she didn't have any—at least, none that fitted her any more. They'd bought three pairs. Mel had near burst with excitement over that one. She wore a pair now.

'A picnic in the botanic gardens,' Princess Melly announced.

'Excellent.' Connor rubbed his hands together, walked her up and down the length of the counter to eye all of Mr Sears's goodies. It was only a touch after eleven o'clock but, given the amount of energy they'd expended already, coupled with the plans he could see racing through Mel's mind, he figured she might need refuelling. 'What should we take on our picnic?'

She stared up at him with big liquid eyes—identical to his, so he was told. He didn't believe it. His eyes couldn't melt a body like that.

'Princess Melly would like a sausage roll now—' she slipped her hand inside his, as if he might need some extra persuasion '—which will spoil her lunch, you know?'

'It will?' He tried to figure out where she was going with this.

'Which means we can just have apple turnovers and lemonade for lunch.'

Connor grinned. Mel's smile slipped. 'Excellent idea,' he assured her. 'Apple turnovers for lunch it is.'

Once in the proverbial blue moon wouldn't hurt, would it?

Her smile beamed out at him again.

Heck, no, it couldn't hurt anything. Still…responsible adult instincts kicked in. 'I am afraid, though, that your humble servant—' he touched his chest '—has a voracious appetite. Would it be permissible for him to order egg-and-lettuce sandwiches to take on the picnic, do you think?'

She nodded solemnly, but her eyes danced. Connor placed their order and they sat at a table in the front window to munch their sausage rolls and sip hot chocolates.

The roar of motorbikes interrupted them mid-bite. They both swung to stare out of the window. Motorbikes—big, black, gleaming Harley-Davidsons—trawled up the street, chrome and leather gleaming in the sun. There had to be at least a dozen bikes, most with pillion passengers…and all the riders wore black leather. Connor blinked, and then he started to laugh, deep and low, and with undeniable satisfaction. The roar and thunder abated as the bikes found parking spaces down either side of the street. All of the leather-clad visitors made a beeline for Jaz's bookshop.

His gut clenched when Jaz danced out to meet them. He thought a blood vessel in his brain might burst when the biggest and burliest of the visitors swung her around as if she didn't weigh any more than a kitten, rather than five feet ten inches of warm, curvaceous woman. When the burly visitor placed her back on the ground, he kissed her on the cheek.

Kissed her! Something dark and ugly pulsed through him.

Jaz hadn't mentioned being involved with anyone in Sydney, but then they hadn't really discussed what she'd been doing since she'd left.

'Daddy?'

He glanced down to find Mel staring at his mangled sausage roll.

He tried to loosen his grip around it, tried to grin. 'Oops, I obviously don't know my own strength.'

Melly giggled.

Connor wiped his hand on a paper serviette and glanced back out of the window. He couldn't stop a replay of all the kisses he and Jaz had shared eight years ago from playing through his mind now—all of them, in all of their endless variety.

He couldn't remember kissing her on the cheek too often.
On the cheek!

That hadn't been the kiss of some lover impatient to see his girlfriend after a week of enforced separation. Connor couldn't explain the rush of relief that poured into him. Actually, he could explain it, but he wouldn't. Not to himself. Not to anyone.

Some of Jaz's friends followed her into the bookshop. Others broke into groups of twos and threes to stroll down whichever side of the street seemed to take their fancy, for all the world like idle tourists. Which was probably what they were. They didn't wear bike gang insignias on their leather jackets. They were probably a bunch of people who shared a passion for bikes. He'd bet they were carpenters and bookshop owners and bakers like him and Jaz and Mr Sears.

He cast a glance around the bakery. He wasn't the only one transfixed. The arrival of over a dozen bikes in town had brought the conversation in the bakery to a screaming halt. Mr

Sears's face had turned the same colour as the icing on his Chelsea buns—pink. Bright pink.

Connor grinned. After the way Mr Sears had treated her this past week, Jaz deserved her revenge. He enjoyed the beauty of her payback. Not that it would boost her popularity rating as far as the rest of the town was concerned. Already an assortment of tourists and locals were surreptitiously returning to their cars and driving away—intimidated by the combination of loud motorbikes and leather.

Then suddenly Jaz was standing outside the Sears's bakery without any of her friends in tow and Connor cursed himself for the distraction that had cost him the treat of watching her stride across the road, head held high and shoulders thrown back. Her eyes met his through the plate glass and that thing arced between them—a combination of heat and history.

The bell above the door tinkled as she entered. 'Hello, Connor.'

'Hello, Jaz.'

She swung away from him abruptly to smile at Mel—an uncomplicated display of pleasure that kicked him in the guts. 'Melly! How are you?'

Melly leaned towards her. 'I'm Princess Melly today.'

Jaz let loose a low whistle. 'Hardly surprising. You do look as pretty as a princess today, you know?'

'Daddy says I look as pretty as a princess every day.' But she said the words uncertainly.

Jaz bent down. 'Princess Melly, I think your daddy is right.' Then she winked. 'By the way, I love the jeans.'

Mel beamed. Connor's gut clenched in consternation. As if she sensed that, Jaz straightened. 'I'd love to stay and chat, but I have visitors to get back to. You have fun today, okay?'

Mel nodded vigorously. 'We will.'

'Hey, Carmen. Howdy, Mr S.' Jaz boomed this last.

Mr Sears raced down to the end of the counter where Jaz stood, the end nearest Connor and Mel. 'What are you doing?'

he demanded in an undertone. 'Trying to chase all of Clara Falls' business out of town?'

'I have nearly twenty people for morning tea.' She didn't lower her voice. 'Which, at least for your bakery, Mr S, is going to be *very* good business. I'll take one of your large carrot cakes, a strawberry sponge and…what would you suggest? A chocolate mud cake or a bee sting?'

Connor couldn't resist. 'Go with the orange and poppy seed, Jaz. It can't be beat.'

She swung around to stare at him. That warmth arced between them again. The colour in her cheeks deepened. Connor's groin kicked to life. She swung back to Mr Sears. 'The orange poppy seed it is.'

Every single one of Mr Sears's muscles—at least those from the waist up that Connor could see—bunched. If steam could've come out of his ears, Connor was guessing it would've. And yet he placed each of the three cakes in a separate cardboard box with the same care and reverence mothers showed to newborn babies.

But when he placed them on the counter for Jaz to collect, he leaned across and grabbed her wrist. Connor pushed his chair back and started to rise.

'If the tone of this town is brought down any further,' Mr Sears hissed, 'you'll ruin the lot of us. And it'll be all your doing.'

'No, it'll be yours,' she returned, as cool as the water in the Clara Falls themselves.

With one twist, she freed her wrist. Connor sat back down. She didn't need his help.

'I run a bookshop, Mr S, and I need to attract customers from somewhere. Until my bookshop starts securing its usual level of trade, and the rumours about drugs trafficking start dying down, I'm afraid you'll have to get used to my weekend visitors. They have bikes and will travel. They believe supporting independent bookshops is a good cause.' She hitched her head in the direction of the door. 'Believe me, this lot is only the tip of the iceberg.'

Mr Sears drew back as if stung.

She sent him what Connor could only call a salacious wink. 'Your call, Mr S.' She lifted the cakes and all but saluted him with them. 'Mighty grateful to you. Have a great day now, you hear? I'll be back later to grab afternoon tea for the hordes. Who knows how many extra bodies could show up between now and then? And those Danish pastries look too good to resist.' With that she swept out of the shop.

A buzz of conversation broke out around the tables the moment the door closed behind her. Connor watched every step of her progress with greedy delight as she returned to the bookshop. She walked as if she owned the whole world. It was sexy as hell. You had to hand it to her. The lady had style.

'Jaz is my friend,' Mel said, hauling his attention back.

He sobered at that. He didn't want his daughter getting too attached to Jaz Harper. It wouldn't do her any good. Just like it hadn't done him any good.

'Stop!'

Luckily Connor had already slowed the car to a crawl in expectation of the approaching pedestrian crossing when Mel shouted, because he planted his foot on the brake immediately.

'What?' He glanced from the left to the right to try and discover what it was that had made Melly shout. Katoomba's main street was crowded with shoppers and tourists alike—a typical Saturday. He couldn't see anything amiss. She couldn't want more food, surely? They'd not long finished their sausage rolls and hot chocolates.

'Jaz just went in there with two of her friends.'

He followed the direction of Mel's finger to Katoomba's one and only tattoo parlour.

Mel lifted her chin. 'I want to go in there too.'

He hesitated. He played for time. He edged the car up to the pedestrian crossing, where he had to wait for pedestrians...and more pedestrians. 'What about the botanic gardens and our picnic?'

'Something is wrong.' Melly's bottom lip wobbled and his gut twisted. 'She looked sad and she's my friend and she made me feel better when I was sad.'

Her bottom lip wobbled some more. He gulped. 'When were you sad?'

'Last week.'

'Why were you sad?'

Would she tell him? He held his breath. The pedestrian crossing cleared and he pushed the car into gear and started moving again.

'Because Mrs Benedict smacked me.'

Connor slid the van into a free parking space and tried to unclench his hands from around the steering wheel. That still had the power to make his blood boil…

But Mel had confided in him!

'You won't ever have to go back to Mrs Benedict's again, okay, sweetheart?'

Mel's eyes went wide, then opaque. Connor couldn't read her face at all. He didn't know if she was about to throw a temper tantrum or burst into tears. 'You said I was Princess Melly today.'

The whispered words speared straight into him. 'You are, sweetheart.'

'And that my every wish was your command.'

'Yep, that's right.' If she didn't want to talk about this, then he wouldn't force her.

'Then I want to see Jaz!'

He was hers to command. But how could he explain that neither one of them had the right to command Jaz?

Why was Jaz sad?

The thought distracted him. Perhaps that was why Mel's escape plan succeeded because, before he realised what she meant to do, she'd slipped off her seat belt, slid out of the car and raced back down the street towards the tattoo parlour.

'Bloody hell!'

Connor shot out of the car after her. He fell through the front door of the tattoo parlour in time to see Mel throw her arms around Jaz's waist as Jaz emerged from the back of the shop.

'What's this?' Jaz hugged Mel back but she glanced up at Connor with a question in her eyes.

'I'm sorry.' He shrugged and grimaced. Mel clung to Jaz like a limpet and an ache burned deep down inside him. 'She got away from me. She saw you and thought you looked sad.' He didn't know what else to say because it suddenly hit him that Mel was right—something was wrong. Jaz was sad. He didn't know how he could tell. Nothing in her bearing gave it away.

Two men emerged from the back of the shop—one of them the man who'd kissed Jaz on the cheek earlier. She smiled at them weakly and shrugged, much the same way he just had to her. 'This is my friend, Melly...and her father Connor. This is Mac and Jeff.'

They all nodded to each other, murmured hellos.

'Melly saw me and wanted to say hello.' She knelt down to Mel's level. 'I am a bit sad, but I promise I'm going to be all right, okay?'

Mel nodded. 'Okay.'

'Now, if you'll excuse me—' Jaz rose '—I have some work to do.'

Connor saw the question forming in Mel's eyes and wanted to clamp a hand over her mouth before she could ask it.

'Are you going to tattoo someone?'

Jaz glanced briefly at him, then back to Mel. 'Yes.'

He wondered why she sounded so reluctant to admit it. One thing was clear—she did not want them here.

Her sadness beat at him like a living thing. He remembered what had happened to Frieda. *She has her friends.*

'Can I watch?'

Jaz crouched back down to Mel's level. 'I don't think that's a good idea, Melly, and—'

'I don't mind.' The man called Jeff spoke quietly, but somehow his words filled the entire room.

'Are you getting the tattoo?' Mel breathed, awe audible in every word.

'I'm getting a picture of my little girl tattooed here.' Jeff touched a hand to the top of his left arm.

'Where is she? Can we play?'

He shook his head. 'She's a long way away.'

Melly bit her lip. 'Is it going to hurt?'

'Yes.'

'Will it help if I hold your hand?'

'Yes, it will.' With a glance at Connor, Jeff picked Melly up in his great burly arms. Connor sensed that with just one word or look from him, Jeff would release Mel in an instant, but something in the man's face and manner, something in the way Jaz regarded him, held Connor still.

Then they all moved to the back of the shop.

The tattoo took nearly two hours. Connor had never seen anything like it in his life. Beneath Jaz's fingers, a young girl's face came alive.

This wasn't just any simple tattoo. It was an indelible photograph captured on this man's arm for ever.

It was a work of art.

Mel watched Jaz's movements quietly, solemnly. She held Jeff's hand, stroked it every now and again. Finally she moved to where Connor sat, slid onto his lap and rested her head against his shoulder. He held her tight, though for the life of him he couldn't explain why. Her relaxed posture and even breathing eventually told him she'd fallen asleep.

At last, Jaz set aside her tools and stretched her arms back above her head. She held up a mirror for Jeff to view the finished tattoo. 'Thank you,' he said simply.

Jaz leant across then and placed a kiss in the centre of Jeff's forehead. 'May she live in your heart for ever,' she whispered.

That was when Connor realised why he held Melly so tight.

That tattoo wasn't a work of art. It was a memorial.

'Cherish her,' Jeff said with a nod at the sleeping child.

'I will,' he promised.

Then Jeff left the room, closely followed by Mac, and Connor expelled one long breath. He reached out and touched Jaz's hand. 'That was the most amazing thing I've ever seen.' He didn't smile. He couldn't. But he wanted her to know how much he admired her skill and generosity.

When she turned, he could see the strain the last two hours had put on her—the overwhelming responsibility to do her absolute best work, not to make a mistake. It showed in her pallor, the lines around her eyes and mouth.

He adjusted the child in his arms, rose and put one arm around Jaz's shoulders. 'Let me take you home.'

For a moment he thought she would lean into him, but then she stiffened and edged away. 'Mac will take me home, thanks all the same. Enjoy the rest of your day, Connor.'

Before she could move fully away, Melly stirred, unwrapped an arm from around her father's neck and wound it around Jaz's. It brought Jaz in close to Connor again—her arm touching his arm, his scent clogging her senses. The more of him she breathed in, the more it chased her weariness away.

'That was way wicked!' Melly said.

A spurt of laughter sprang from Jaz's lips at the sheer un-expectedness of Melly's words. She tried to draw back a little to stare into Melly's face. Melly wouldn't let her draw back any further than that. 'Where did you pick up that expression?'

'Carmen Sears. She looked after me for a couple of hours yesterday and I think she's way wicked too.'

Jaz grinned. She couldn't help it. Although she kept her gaze on Melly's face, from the corner of her eye she could see Connor's lips kick up too. Her heart pounded against the walls of her chest as if her ribcage had shrunk.

'Can we go on our picnic now, Daddy?'

'Your wish is my command.'

'I want Jaz to come on our picnic too.'

Jaz stiffened. She tried to draw away but Melly tightened her hold and wouldn't let her go. Oh, heck! Connor had told her he didn't want her as part of Melly's life. She should imagine that included attending picnics with her.

'Princess, your wish is *my* every command,' Connor started.

'You're going to say no.'

Melly's bottom lip wobbled. It wouldn't have had such a profound effect on Jaz if she hadn't sensed Melly's valiant effort to hide it. Connor's Adam's apple bobbed.

'Sweetheart, Jaz isn't anyone's to command. She's her own princess. We don't have the right to tell her what to do.'

Mel leaned in close to her father and whispered, 'But Jaz might like to come.'

He hesitated. He nodded. Then he smiled. 'I guess you'd better ask her, then.'

'Princess Jaz, would you like to come on a picnic with us?' She turned pleading eyes on Jaz. 'Please?'

Thank you, Connor Reed! So she had to play bad guy, huh? She wondered if she could lie convincingly enough not to hurt Melly's feelings. The hope in the child's face turned Jaz's insides to…marshmallow.

'I would love to come on a picnic with you, Princess Melly…' That wasn't a lie. 'But I'm very tired.' That wasn't a lie either. 'And I really should get back to the bookshop.' That was only half a lie.

'But you're still sad!'

Melly's grip eased, but she didn't let go. Her bottom lip wobbled again, making Jaz gulp. If Melly cried…

'Please come along with us, Jaz.'

Connor's voice, warm and golden, slid through to her very core. Her decidedly marshmallow core.

'I'd like you to come along too.'

She had to meet his gaze. Those words, that tone, demanded it. Her breath hitched. His autumn-tinted eyes tempted her…in every way possible.

She shouldn't go.

He couldn't really want her to tag along.

'Bonnie and Gail have the shop under control,' Mac said from the doorway. 'Go on the picnic, Jaz, it'll do you good.'

Three sets of eyes watched her expectantly. 'I…' Exhilaration raced through her veins. 'I think a picnic sounds perfect.'

'Good.'

If anything, Connor's eyes grew warmer.

Oh, dear Lord. What had she just agreed to?

Melly struggled out of her father's arms to throw her arms around Jaz's middle. 'Yay! Thank you.'

She smoothed Melly's hair back behind her ears. 'No, sweet-heart, *thank you* for inviting me along. It'll be a real treat.'

She glanced up at Connor and for some reason her tongue tried to stick fast to the roof of her mouth. 'I'll…umm…just go grab my things.'

In the end, Melly decided it was too far to go to the botanic gardens and chose a picnic spot near Katoomba Cascades instead. Jaz couldn't remember a time when egg-and-lettuce sandwiches or apple turnovers had tasted so good.

After they'd eaten, they walked down to the cascades. The day was still and clear and cool. Jaz drank in the scenery like a starving woman. She hadn't forgotten how beautiful the mountains were, but her recollections had been overshadowed by…other memories.

Melly's chatter subsided abruptly when they returned to the picnic area. She stared at the children playing in the play-ground—two swings, a tiny fort with a climbing frame and a slippery dip—and the hunger in her face made Jaz's heart twist.

Melly swung around, her gaze spearing straight to Jaz's, a question in her eyes that brought Jaz's childhood crashing back—the crippling shyness…the crippling loneliness.

She made herself smile, nodded towards the playground. 'Why don't you go over and make friends?' Then she remembered Connor. Not that she'd ever forgotten him. 'We don't have to go home yet, do we?'

'This is Princess Melly day.' He spread his arms as if that said it all.

Jaz wished he hadn't spread his arms quite so wide or in that particular fashion. If she took just one step towards him she'd find herself encompassed by those arms.

A small hand slipped inside Jaz's, hauling her back. Melly stared up at her with such trust in her autumn-tinted eyes—eyes the spitting image of Connor's—that it stole her breath.

'But what do I say?' Melly whispered.

Jaz dropped her duffel bag to the grass and knelt down beside Melly. She took a second look at the children playing in the playground. Tourists. 'I think you should go over and say: Hello, I'm Melly and I live near here. Where do you live? And then…' Jaz racked her brain. She remembered her own childhood. She could sense Connor watching them intently, but she did what she could to ignore him for the moment. 'Remember that story we read—was it Tuesday or Wednesday? The one with the wood sprites and the water nymphs.'

Melly nodded.

'Well, perhaps you could tell them about the wood sprites and water nymphs that live in the Katoomba Cascades.' She nodded her head in the direction of the cascades. 'I'm sure they'd love to hear about that.'

Melly's face lit up. 'Can I go play, Daddy?'

He spread his arms again. It made Jaz gulp. 'Is your name Princess Melly?'

Melly giggled and raced off.

Connor lowered himself to the grass beside Jaz, stretched out on his side. 'Thank you.'

'I…' Her tongue had gone and glued itself to the roof of her mouth again.

'You said exactly the right thing.' He frowned. 'How'd you do that?'

Her tongue unglued itself. 'Why, what would you have said?'

'I'd have probably told her to just play it by ear.'

Jaz shook her head. 'I remember what it was like to be Melanie's age…and shy. I'd have wanted some clear instructions or suggestions about how to get the initial conversation started. You can play it by ear after that.'

Connor watched Melly. 'It seems to be working.'

Warmth wormed through her. 'I'm glad. She's a delightful little girl, Connor. You must be very proud of her.'

He glanced up at her. 'I am.'

She gripped her hands together. 'I'm sorry I came along today,' she blurted out. But it was partly his fault. He'd caught her at a weak moment.

He shot up into a sitting position. 'Why?' he barked. 'Haven't you had a nice time?'

'Yes, of course, but…' She stared back at him helplessly. 'But you didn't want me as part of Melly's life, remember? I was supposed to keep my distance.' She lifted her hands, then let them fall back to her lap. 'But I didn't know how to say no to her.' She glared. 'And you didn't help.'

She didn't know if it was a grimace or a smile that twisted his lips. 'She wanted you to come along so badly. I didn't know how to say no to her either.'

What about him? Had he really wanted her to come along?

She halted that thought in its tracks. She didn't care what Connor wanted.

'I seem to recall you saying you didn't want me as part of your life either.'

She wrinkled her nose. 'That was just me wanting to say something mean back to you.' It had been about erecting defences.

'It wasn't mean. It was you telling the truth, wasn't it?'

She had no intention of letting him breach those defences. 'Yes.' She pulled in a breath. 'There's a lot of history between us, Connor.'

He nodded.

'And I have no intention of revisiting it.'

'History never repeats?' he asked.

'Something like that.'

'For what it's worth, I think you're right.' He was quiet for a long moment, his eyes on Melly. 'It doesn't mean you and Mel can't be friends, though, does it?'

She blinked. 'But you didn't want me to…'

'For better or worse, Melly likes you, she identifies with you.' He met her gaze head-on. 'But can you promise me that you won't leave again the way you did the last time?'

'Yes, I can promise that.' She'd grown up since those days. 'It's funny, you know, but it's nice to be back.' She gestured to the view spread out before them. 'I've missed all this. When I do get the bookshop back on its feet, I mean to come back for visits.'

She'd promised Gwen.

She'd promise Melly too.

'I have no intention of hurting your little girl, Connor.'

'I know that.'

She turned and stared back out at the view.

CHAPTER SEVEN

THE hunger in Jaz's face as she stared out over the valley made Connor's gut clench.

This was her home. She might not be ready to admit that to herself yet, but the truth was as clear to him as the nose on her face…and the fullness of her lips.

He tried to drag his mind from her lips, from thoughts of kissing her. Jaz had made her position clear—there would be no him and her again.

He didn't know why that should make him scowl. It was what he wanted too.

No, he wanted to kiss her. He was honest enough to admit that much. But she was right. There was no future for them.

But now that she was back in Clara Falls, she shouldn't have to leave in twelve months' time. Not if she didn't want to.

He thought back to Mac—the cheek kisser; Mac of the tattoo parlour. He rolled his shoulders. 'You're good with kids.' Did she plan to have children of her own?

She turned back. He could tell she was trying to hold back a grin. 'You sound surprised.'

'Guess I've never really thought about it before.' He paused. 'You and Mac seem close.'

Her lips twisted. She all but cocked an eyebrow. 'We are. He and his wife Bonnie are my best friends.'

He felt like a transparent fool. He rushed on before she

could chide him for getting too personal. 'What are your plans for when you return to your real life in the city?'

She blinked and he shrugged, suddenly and strangely self-conscious—like Mel in her attempts to make new friends. 'You said that returning to run the bookshop was a temporary glitch.'

'It is.'

She eased back on her hands, shifted so she no longer sat on her knees, so she could stretch the long length of her legs out in front of her. Without thinking, he reached out to swipe the leaves from her trouser legs.

She stiffened. He pulled his hand back with a muttered, 'Sorry.'

'Not a problem.'

Her voice came out all tight and strangled. Oh, yeah, there was a problem all right. The same problem there had always been between them—that heat. But it hadn't solved things between them eight years ago and it wouldn't solve anything now.

He just had to remember not to touch her.

'Your plans?' he prompted when she didn't unstiffen.

'Oh, yes.' She relaxed. She waved to Melly on the slippery dip. She didn't look at him; she stared out at the view—it was a spectacular view. He didn't know if her nonchalance was feigned or not, but it helped ease the tenseness inside him a little—enough for him to catch his breath.

He made himself stare out at the view too. It *was* spectacular.

Not as spectacular—

Don't go there.

'I mean to open an art gallery.'

He stared at her. Every muscle in his body tensed up again. 'An art gallery?' An ache stretched through him. He ignored it. 'But don't you run a tattoo parlour?'

'And a bookshop,' she reminded him.

She smiled. Not at him but at something she saw in the middle distance. 'Mac and I financed the tattoo parlour together, but Mac is the one in charge of its day-to-day running. I'm more of a…guest artist.'

The thought made him smile.

'I'm pretty much a silent partner these days.'

'Perhaps that's what you need at the bookshop—a partner?'

She swung around. 'I hadn't thought of that.' Then, 'No.' She gave a decisive shake of her head. 'The bookshop is all I have left of my mother.'

'And you don't want to share?'

Her eyes became hooded. 'It's my responsibility, that's all.' She turned back to the view.

'So the art gallery, that would be your real baby?'

She lifted one shoulder. 'I guess.'

'Where are planning to set it up?'

'I'd only just started looking for premises when Mum—' She broke off. His heart burned in sympathy.

'I found wonderful premises at Bondi Beach.'

Despite the brightness of her voice, her pain slid in beneath his skin like a splinter of polished hardwood. He wanted to reach for her, only he knew she wouldn't accept his comfort.

He clenched his hands. 'Bondi?' He tried to match her brightness.

'Yes, but I'm afraid the rent went well beyond my budget.'

'I bet.' It suddenly occurred to him that the rents in the Blue Mountains weren't anywhere near as exorbitant as those in the city.

'An art gallery...' He couldn't finish the sentence. All the brightness had drained from his voice. He could see her running this hypothetical gallery, could almost taste her enthusiasm and drive. He could see her paintings hanging on the walls. He could—

'Which brings me to another point.' She turned. Her eyes burned in her face as she fixed him with a glare. 'You!'

He stared back. Somewhere in the background he heard Melly's laughter, registered that she was safe and happy at the moment. 'Me?' What had he done?

She dragged her duffel bag towards her. The bag she'd refused to leave in the car. The one she hadn't allowed him to carry for her on their walk. She'd treated it as if it contained something precious. He'd thought it must hold her tattooing gear. He blinked when she slapped something down on his knees.

A sketch pad!

Bile rose up through him when she pushed a pencil into his hand. 'Draw, Connor.'

Panic gripped him.

She opened the sketch pad. 'Draw,' she ordered again.

She reached over and shook his hand, the one that held the pencil, and he went cold all over.

'No!'

He tried to rise, but she grabbed hold of his arm and wouldn't let it go.

'I don't draw any more,' he ground out, trying to beat back the darkness that threatened him.

'Nonsense!'

'For pity's sake, Jaz, I—'

'You're scared.'

It was a taunt, a challenge. It made him grit his teeth together in frustration. His fingers around the pencil felt as fat and useless as sausages. 'I gave it up,' he ground out.

'Then it's time you took it back up again.'

Anger shot through him. 'You want to see how bad I've become, is that what this is about?' Did she want some kind of sick triumph over him?

Her eyes travelled across his face. Her chin lifted. 'If that's what it takes.'

Then her eyes became gentle and it was like a punch to the gut. 'Please?' she whispered.

All he could smell was the sweet scent of wattle.

He gripped the pencil so hard it should've snapped. If she wanted him to draw, then he'd draw. Maybe when she saw how ham-fisted he'd become she'd finally leave him in peace. 'What do you want me to draw?'

'That tree.' She pointed.

Connor studied it for a moment—its scale, the dimensions.

They settled automatically into his mind. That quick summing up, it was one of the things that made him such a good builder. But he didn't deceive himself. He had no hope of being a halfway decent artist any more.

It didn't mean he wanted Jaz forcing that evidence in front of him. She sat beside him, arms folded, and an air of expectation hung about her. He knew he could shake her off with ease and simply walk away, but such an action would betray the importance he placed on this simple act of drawing.

He dragged a hand down his face. Failure now meant the death of something good deep down inside him. If Jaz sensed how much it meant—and he had the distinct impression she knew exactly what it meant—he had no intention of revealing it by storming away from her. He'd face failure with grace.

Maybe, when this vain attempt was over, the restlessness that plagued him on bright, still days would disappear. His lips twisted. They said there was a silver lining in every cloud, didn't they?

Just when he sensed Jaz's impatience had become too much for her, he set pencil to paper.

And failed.

He couldn't draw any more. The lines he made were too heavy, the sense of balance and perspective all wrong...no flow. He tried to tell himself he'd expected it, but darkness pressed against the backs of his eyes. Jaz peered across at what he'd done and he had to fight the urge to hunch over it and hide it from her sight.

She tore the page from the sketch pad, screwed it into a ball and set it on the ground beside her. Sourness filled his mouth. He'd tried to tell her.

'Draw the playground.'

He gaped at her.

She shrugged. 'Well...what are you waiting for?' She waved to Melly again.

Was she being deliberately obtuse? He stared at the playground, with all its primary colours. The shriek of Melly's laughter filled the air, and that ache pressed against him harder. In a former life he'd have painted that in such brilliant colours it would steal one's breath.

But that was then.

He set pencil to paper again but his fingers refused to follow the dictates of his brain. He'd turned his back on art to become a carpenter. It only seemed right that his fingers had turned into blocks of wood. Nevertheless, he kept trying because he knew Jaz didn't want to triumph over him. She wanted him to draw again—to know its joys, its freedoms once more…to bow to its demands and feel whole.

When she discovered he could no longer draw, she would mourn that loss as deeply as he did.

When he finally put the pencil down, she peeled the page from the sketch pad…and that drawing followed the same fate as its predecessor—screwed up and set down beside her.

'Draw that rock with the clump of grass growing around it.'

He had to turn ninety degrees but it didn't matter. A different position did not bring any latent talent to the fore.

She screwed that picture up too when he was finished with it. Frustration started to oust his sense of defeat. 'Look, Jaz, I—'

'Draw the skyway.'

It meant turning another ninety degrees. 'What's the point?' he burst out. 'I—'

She pushed him—physically. Anger balled in the pit of his stomach.

'Stop your whining,' she snapped.

His hands clenched. 'You push me again…'

'And you'll what?' she taunted.

He flung the sketch pad aside. 'I've had enough!'

'Well, I haven't!' She retrieved the sketch pad and slapped it back on his knees. 'Draw the skyway, Connor!'

Draw the skyway? He wished he were out on that darn skyway right now!

His fingers flew across the page. The sooner this was over, the better. He didn't glance at the drawing when he'd finished. He just tossed the sketch pad at Jaz, not caring if she caught it or not.

She did catch it. And she stared at it for a long, long time. Bile rose from his stomach to burn his throat.

'Better,' she finally said. She didn't tear it from the sketch pad. She didn't screw it up into a ball.

'Don't humour me, Jaz.' The words scraped out of his throat, raw with emotion, but he didn't care. He could deal with defeat but he would not stand for her pity.

In answer, she gave him one of the balled rejects. 'Look at it.'

He was too tired to argue. He smoothed it out and grimaced. It was the picture of the playground. It was dreadful, horrible…a travesty.

'No,' she said when he went to ball it up again. 'Look at it.'

He looked at it.

'Now look at this.' She stood up and held his drawing of the skyway in front of her.

Everything inside him stilled. It was flawed, vitally flawed in a lot of respects, and yet… He'd captured something there—a sense of freedom and escape. Jaz was right. It was better.

Was it enough of an improvement to count, though?

He glanced up into her face. She pursed her lips and surveyed where he sat. 'This is all wrong.' She tapped a finger against her chin for a moment, then her face cleared. She seized her duffel bag. 'Come with me.'

She led him to a nearby stand of trees. He followed her. His heart thudded in his chest, part of him wanted to turn tail and run, but he followed.

'Sit there.'

She pointed to the base of a tree. Its position would still give him a good, clear view of Melly playing. Melly waved. He waved back.

He settled himself against the tree.

'Good.' She handed him the sketch pad and pencil again. She

pulled a second sketch pad and more pencils from her bag and settled herself on the ground to his left, legs crossed. She looked so familiar, hunched over like that, Connor thought he'd been transported back eight years in time.

She glanced across at him. 'Bend your knees like you used to do…as if you're sitting against that old tree at our lookout.'

Our lookout. Richardson's Peak—out of the way and rarely visited. They'd always called it *their lookout.* He tried to hold back the memories.

Jaz touched a hand to the ground. 'See, I'm sitting on the nearby rock.'

It wasn't rock. It was grass, but Connor gave in, adjusted his back and legs, and let the memories flood through him. 'What do you want me to draw?'

'The view.'

Panoramas had always been his speciality, but he wasn't quite sure where to start now.

He wasn't convinced that this wasn't a waste of time.

'Close your eyes.'

She whispered the command. She closed her eyes so he closed his eyes too. It might shut out the ache that gripped him whenever he looked at her.

It didn't, but her voice washed over him, soft and low, soothing him. 'Remember what it was like at the lookout?' she murmured. 'The grand vista spread out in front of us and the calls of the birds…the scent of eucalyptus in the air…'

All Connor could smell was wattle, and he loved it, dragged it into his lungs greedily.

'Remember how the sun glinted off the leaves, how it warmed us in our sheltered little spot, even when the wind played havoc with everything else around us?'

His skin grew warm, his fingers relaxed around the pencil.

'Now draw,' she whispered.

He opened his eyes and drew.

On the few occasions he glanced across at her, he found her

hunched over her sketch pad, her fingers moving with the same slow deliberation he remembered from his dreams.

Time passed. Connor had no idea how long they drew but, when he finally set aside his pencil, he glanced up to find the shadows had lengthened and Jaz waiting for him. He searched the picnic ground for Melly.

'Just over there.' Jaz nodded and he found Melly sitting on the grass with her new friends.

'Finished?' she asked.

He nodded.

'May I see?'

She asked in the same shy way she'd have asked eight years ago. He smiled. He felt tired and alive and…free. 'If you want.'

She was by his side in a second. She turned back to the first page in the sketch pad. He'd lost count of how many pictures he'd drawn. His fingers had flown as if they'd had to make up for the past eight years of shackled inactivity.

Jaz sighed and chuckled and teased him, just like she used to do. She pointed to one of the drawings and laughed. 'Is that supposed to be a bird?'

'I was trying to give the impression of time flying.'

'It needs work,' she said with a grin.

He returned her grin. 'So do my slippery dips.'

'Yep, they do.'

The laughter in her voice lifted him.

'But look at how you've captured the way the light shines through the trees here. It's beautiful.'

She turned her face to meet his gaze fully and light trembled in her eyes. 'You can draw again, Connor.'

Her exultation reached out and wrapped around him. *He could draw again.*

He couldn't help himself. He cupped one hand around the back of her head, threaded his fingers through her hair and drew her lips down to his and kissed her—warm, firm…brief. Then he released her because he knew he couldn't take too much of that. 'Thank you. If you hadn't badgered me…' He gestured to the sketch pad.

She drew back, her eyes wide and dazed. 'You're welcome, but—' she moistened her lips '—I didn't do much.'

Didn't do much.

'You had it in you all the time. You just had to let it out, that's all.' She reached up, touched her fingers to her lips. She pulled them away again when she realised he watched her. Her breathing had quickened, grown shallow. She lifted her chin and glared at him. 'If you ever turn your back on your gift again, it will desert you. For ever!'

He knew she was right.

He knew he wanted to kiss her again.

As if she'd read that thought in his face, Jaz drew back. 'It's getting late. We'd better start thinking about making tracks.'

She didn't want him to kiss her.

He remembered all the reasons why he shouldn't kiss her. 'You're right.'

He tried to tell himself it was for the best.

Jaz found Connor sitting on the sales counter munching what looked like a Danish pastry when she let herself into the bookshop at eight o'clock on Monday morning.

'Hey, Jaz.'

She blinked. 'Hello.'

What was he doing here? Shouldn't he be upstairs working on her flat? The absence of hammering and sawing suddenly registered. Her heart gave a funny little leap. 'Is my flat ready?'

'We're completing the final touches today and tomorrow, and then it'll be ready for the painters and carpet layers.'

She'd already decided to paint it herself. It'd give her something to do. Funnily enough, though, considering how she'd expected her time in Clara Falls to drag, this last week had flown.

She'd have the carpet laid in double-quick time. She wasn't spending winter in the mountains on bare floorboards. Once her furniture was delivered from Connor's, she could paint and decorate the flat in her own good time.

She edged around behind the counter to place her handbag in one of the drawers and tried to keep Connor's scent from addling her brain. Handbag taken care of, she edged back out again—his scent too evocative, too tempting. It reminded her of that kiss. That brief thank you of a kiss that had seared her senses.

Forget about the kiss.

'Did you want me for something?'

His eyes darkened at her words and her mouth went dry. He slid off the counter and moved towards her—a hunter stalking its prey. He wore such a look of naked intensity that... Good Lord! He didn't mean to kiss her again, did he? She wanted to turn and flee but her legs wouldn't work. He reached out...took her hand...and...

And plonked a paper bag into it.

'I thought you might like one.'

Like one...? She glanced into the bag. A pastry—he'd given her a pastry. In fact, he'd handed her a whole bag full of them. 'There's at least a dozen pastries in here.'

'Couldn't remember what filling you preferred.'

She almost called him a liar. Then remembered her manners. And her common sense. Who knew how much he'd forgotten in eight years?

But once upon a time he'd teased her about her apple pie tastes. She wished she could forget.

Her hand inched into the bag for an apple Danish. She pulled it back at the last moment. 'I don't want a pastry!'

She wanted Connor and his disturbing presence and soul-aching scent out of her shop. She tossed the bag of Danishes onto the counter with an insouciance that would've made Mr Sears blanch. 'Why are you here, Connor? What do you want?'

'I want to thank you.'

'For?'

'For your advice to me about Melly. For making me draw again.'

He'd already thanked her for that—*with a kiss!*

She didn't want that kind of thanks, thank you very much. Her heart thud-thudded at the thought of a repeat performance, calling her a liar.

'I think I've made a start on winning back Mel's trust.'

'If Saturday's evidence is anything to go by, I think you're right.' And she was glad for him.

Glad for Melly, she amended.

Okay—she shifted her weight from one foot to the other, slid her hands into the pockets of her trousers—she was glad for both of them, but she was gladder for Melly.

'Look, Jaz, I've been thinking…'

Her mouth went dry. Something in his tone… 'About?'

'What if you didn't leave Clara Falls at the end of this twelve months?'

Her jaw dropped.

He raised both hands. 'Now hear me out before you start arguing.'

She supposed she'd have to because she appeared to have lost all power of speech.

'What if you opened your art gallery in the mountains? It has two advantages over the city. One—lower rents. And two— you'd get the passing tourist trade.' He spread his arms in *that* way. 'Surely that has to be good.'

Of course it was good, but—

'There's an even bigger tourist trade in Sydney,' she pointed out.

'And you'll only attract them if you find premises on or around the harbour.'

She could never afford that.

'What's more, if you settle around here you'll be close to the bookshop if you're needed, and it's an easy commute to the city on the days you're needed in at the tattoo parlour.'

He spread his arms again. 'If you think about it, it makes perfect sense.'

'No, it doesn't!'

He didn't look the least fazed by her outburst. 'Sure it does. And, Jaz, Clara Falls needs people like you.'

She gaped at him then. 'It's official—Connor Reed has rocks in his head.' She stalked through the shop to the kitchenette. 'People like me?' She snorted. 'Get real!'

'People who aren't afraid of hard work,' Connor said right behind her. 'People who care.'

'You're pinning the wrong traits on the wrong girl.' She seized the jug and filled it.

He leant his hip against the sink. 'I don't think so. In fact, I know I'm not.'

She would not look into those autumn-tinted eyes. After a moment's hesitation, she lifted a mug in his direction in a silent question. Common courtesy demanded she at least offer him coffee. After all, he had supplied the pastries.

'Love one,' he said with that infuriating cheerfulness that set her teeth on edge.

He didn't speak while she made the coffees. She handed him one and made the mistake of glancing into those eyes. Things inside her heated up and melted down, turned to mush.

No mush, she ordered.

That didn't work so she dragged her gaze away to stare out of the window.

'Clara Falls needs you, Jaz.'

'But I don't need Clara Falls.'

He remained silent for so long that she finally turned and met his gaze. The gentleness in his eyes made her swallow.

'That's where I think you're wrong. I think you need Clara Falls as much as you ever did. I think you're still searching for the same security, the same acceptance now as you did when you were a teenager.'

Very carefully, she set her coffee down because throwing it

all over Connor would be very poor form…and dangerous. The coffee was hot. Very hot. 'You have no idea what you're talking about.'

'You might not want to admit it, but you know I'm right.'

'Garbage! You're the guy with rocks in his head, remember?'

'Frieda knew it too. It's why she wanted you to come back.'

Her mother's name was like a punch to the solar plexus. She wanted to swing away but there wasn't much swinging room in the kitchenette, and to leave meant walking—squeezing— past Connor. If he tried to prevent her from leaving, it would bring them slam-bang up against each other—chest-to-chest, thigh-to-thigh. She wasn't risking that.

She tossed her head. 'How do you know what my mother thought?'

He glanced down into his coffee and it hit her then. 'You…the pair of you talked about me…behind my back?'

'We'd have been happy to do it to your face, Jaz, if you'd ever bothered to come back.'

Guilt swamped her. And regret. How could she have put her mother through so much? Frieda had only ever wanted Jaz's happiness. Jaz had returned that love by refusing to set foot back in Clara Falls. She'd returned that love by breaking her mother's heart.

Connor swore at whatever he saw in her face. He set his mug down and took a step towards her. Jaz seized her coffee, held it in a gesture that warned him he'd wear it if he took another step. 'Don't even think about it!' If he touched her, she'd cry. She would not cry in front of him.

He settled back against the sink.

'I know I am responsible for my mother's death, Connor. Rubbing my nose in that fact, though, hardly seems the friendly thing to do.'

Frown lines dug furrows into his forehead, drew his eyebrows down low over his eyes. 'What the hell…! You are not responsible for Frieda's suicide.'

He believed that, she could tell. She lifted her chin. He could believe what he liked. She knew the truth.

He straightened. 'Jaz, I—'

'I don't particularly want to talk about this, Connor. And, frankly, no offence intended, but nothing you say will make the slightest scrap of difference.'

'How big are you going to let that chip on your shoulder grow before you let it bury you?'

'Chip?' Her mouth opened and closed but no other words would emerge.

'Fine, we won't talk about your mother, but we will talk about Clara Falls and the possibility of you staying on.'

'There is no possibility. It's not going to happen so just give it a rest.'

'You're not giving yourself or the town the slightest chance on this, Jaz. How fair is that?'

Fair? This had nothing to do with fair. This had to do with putting the past behind her.

'Have you come back to save your mother's shop? Or to damn it?'

How could he even ask her that?

'You need to start getting involved in the local community if you mean to save it. Even if you are only here for twelve months.'

She didn't have to do any such thing.

'The book fair is a start.'

He knew about—?

'You've done a great job on the posters.'

Oh, yes.

'But you need to let the local people see that you're not still the rebel Goth girl.'

Darn it! He had a point. She didn't want to admit it but he did have a point.

'You need to show people that you're all grown up, that you're a confident and capable businesswoman now.'

Was that how he saw her?

She dragged her hands back through her hair to help her think, but as Connor followed that action she wished she'd left her hands exactly where they were. Memories pounded at her. She remembered the way he used to run his fingers through her hair, the way he'd massaged her scalp, how it had soothed and seduced at the same time. And being a confident and capable businesswoman didn't seem any defence at all.

'The annual Harvest Ball is next Saturday night. I dare you to come as my date.'

He folded his arms. His eyes twinkled. He looked good enough to eat. She tried to focus her mind on what he'd said rather than…other things. 'Why?' Why did he want to take her to the ball?

'It'll reintroduce you to the local community, for a start, but also…it occurred to me that while it's all well and good for me to preach to you about staying here in Clara Falls and making it a better place, I should be doing that too. I think it's time Mr Sears had some competition for that councillor's spot, don't you?'

She stared at him. 'You're going to run for town councillor?'

'Yep.'

Being seen with her, taking her to the ball, would make a definite statement about what he believed in, about the kind of town he wanted Clara Falls to be. Going to the ball would help her quash nasty rumours about drugs and whatnot too.

'Our going to the ball…' she moistened her lips '…that would be business, right?'

She'd made her position clear on Saturday during the picnic. He'd agreed—history didn't repeat. For some reason, though, she needed to double-check.

'That's right.' He frowned. 'What else would it be?'

'N…nothing.'

The picture of Frieda she'd started on the bookshop's wall grew large in her mind. The darn picture she couldn't seem to finish. *Have you come back to save your mother's shop? Or to damn it?*

She wanted to save it. She had to save it.

She shot out her hand. 'I'll take you up on that dare.'

He clasped her hand in warm work-roughened fingers. Then he bent down and kissed her cheek, drenched her in his scent and his heat. 'Good,' he said softly. 'I'll pick you up at seven next Saturday evening.'

'Well—' she reclaimed her hand, smoothed down the front of her trousers '—I guess that's settled, then. Oh! Except I'm going to need more of my things.' Something formal to wear for a start and her strappy heels.

'Why don't I run you around to my place after work this afternoon and you can pick out what you need?'

'Are you sure?' She wasn't a hundred per cent certain what she meant by that only…she remembered the way he hadn't wanted her at his home last week. She added a quick, 'You're not busy?'

'No. And I've arranged for Carmen to mind Mel for a couple of hours this afternoon.'

Had he been so certain she'd say yes?

You did say yes.

She moistened her lips again. 'Thank you, I'd appreciate that.'

She didn't bother trying to stifle the curiosity that balled inside her. She just hoped it didn't show. It didn't make any sense, but she was dying to know where Connor lived now. Not that it had anything to do with her, of course.

Of course it didn't.

'I'll pick you up about five-fifteen this afternoon.'

Then he was gone.

Jaz reached up and touched her cheek. The imprint of his lips still burned there. A business arrangement, she told herself. That was all this was—a business arrangement.

Jaz slipped into the car the moment Connor pulled it to a halt outside the bookshop. At precisely five-fifteen.

'Hi.'

'Hi.'

That was the sum total of their conversation.

Until he swung the car into the drive of Rose Cottage approximately three minutes later and turned off the ignition. 'Here we are,' he finally said.

She gaped at him. She turned back to stare at the house. 'You bought Rose Cottage?'

Most old towns had a Rose Cottage, and as a teenager Jaz had coveted this one. Single-storey sandstone, wide verandas, established gardens, roses lining the drive, picket fence—it had been her ideal of the perfect family home.

It still was.

And now it belonged to Connor? A low whistle left her. Business must be booming if he could afford this. 'You bought Rose Cottage,' she repeated. He'd known how she'd felt about it.

'That's right.' His face had shuttered, closed.

Had he bought it because of her or in spite of her?

'Your things are in there.'

She dragged her gaze from the house to follow the line of his finger to an enormous garage.

He wasn't going to invite her inside the house?

She glanced into his face and her anticipation faded. He had no intention of inviting her inside, of giving her the grand tour. She swallowed back a lump of disappointment…and a bigger lump of hurt. The disappointment she could explain. She did what she could to ignore the hurt.

'Shall we go find what you need?'

'Yes, thank you, that would be lovely.'

She followed him into the garage, blinked when he flicked a switch and flooded the cavernous space with stark white light. Her things stood on the left and hardly took up any space at all. 'All I need is—'

She stopped short. Then veered off in the opposite direction.

'Jaz, your stuff is over here!'

She heard him, but she couldn't heed his unspoken command. She couldn't stop.

Her feet did slow, though, as she moved along the aisle of handmade wood-turned furniture that stood there—writing desks, coffee tables, chests. She marvelled at their craftsmanship, at the attention paid to detail, at the absolute perfection of each piece.

'You made these?'

'Yes.'

The word left him, clipped and short.

He didn't need to explain. Jaz understood immediately. This was what he'd thrown himself into when he'd given up his drawing and painting.

'Connor, you didn't give up your art. You just…redirected it.'

He didn't say anything.

'These pieces are amazing, beautiful.' She knelt down in front of a wine rack, reached out and trailed her fingers across the wood. 'You've been selling some of these pieces to boutiques in Sydney, haven't you?'

'Yes.'

'I came across a piece similar to this a couple of years back.' She forced herself upright. If she'd known then that Connor had made it she'd have moved heaven and earth to buy it.

'I went into that shop in my lunch hour every day for a week just to look at it.'

His face lost some of its hardness. 'Did you buy it?'

'No.' It had been beyond her budget. 'I couldn't justify the expense at the time.'

She sensed his disappointment, though she couldn't say how—the set of his shoulders or his lips, perhaps?

'Mind you,' she started conversationally, 'it did take a whole week of lecturing myself to be sensible… and if it had been that gorgeous bookcase—' she motioned across to the next piece '—I'd have been lost…and horrendously in debt. Which is why I'm going to back away from it now, nice and slow.'

Finally he smiled back at her.

'My things!' She suddenly remembered why they were here. 'I'll just grab them and get out of your hair.'

He didn't urge her to take her time. He didn't offer to show her any of the other marvels lined up in the garage. She told herself she was a fool for hoping that he would.

CHAPTER EIGHT

WHEN Jaz opened the door to him on Saturday evening, Connor's jaw nearly hit the ground. She stood there in a floor-length purple dress and he swore he'd never seen anything more perfect in his life. The dress draped the lines of her body in Grecian style folds to fasten between her breasts with a diamanté brooch. It oozed elegance and sex appeal. It suited the confident, capable businesswoman she'd become.

Ha! No, it didn't. Not in this lifetime. That dress did not scream professional businesswoman. The material flowed and ran over her body in a way that had his hands itching and his skin growing too tight for the rest of his body. It definitely wasn't businesslike. What he wanted to do to Jaz in that dress definitely wasn't businesslike.

He had to remind himself that the only kind of relationship Jaz wanted with him these days was businesslike.

He had to remind himself that that was what he wanted too.

'Hi, Connor.'

Gwen waved to him from the end of the hallway. It made him realise that he and Jaz hadn't spoken a word to each other yet. He took in Jaz's heightened colour, noted how her eyes glittered with an awareness that matched his own, and desire fireballed in his groin. If they were alone, he'd back her up against a wall, mould each one of her delectable curves to the angles of his body and slake his hunger in the wet shine of her lips.

No, he wouldn't!

Bloody hell. *Get a grip, man. This is a business arrangement.* He tried to spell out the word in his head—B-U-S… It was a sort of business arrangement, he amended. He wanted to help Jaz the way she'd helped him. He wanted to prove to her that Clara Falls was more than Mr Sears and his pointed conservatism. He wanted her to see the good here—the way Frieda had. Instinct told him Jaz needed to do at least that much. If she wanted to leave at the end of twelve months after that, then all power to her.

He glanced down into her face and tried to harden himself against the soft promise of her lips…and the lush promise of her body.

Gwen strode down the hallway. 'Are you okay, Connor?'

He realised he still hadn't uttered a word. 'Uh…' He cleared his throat, ran a finger around the inside collar of his dress shirt. 'These things cut a man's windpipe in two. I feel as trussed up as a Sunday roast.'

'You look damn fine in it, though.'

'You're looking pretty stunning yourself,' manners made him shoot back at her. In truth, with Jaz in the same room he barely saw Gwen. He had a vague impression of red and that was about it.

Jaz folded her arms and glared at him. Man, what had he done now? He turned back to Gwen. 'Who's your date tonight, then?'

Gwen shook her head. 'I'm going stag this year. I don't want to be shackled to any man. Not when there'll be so many eligible males to choose from this evening.'

Fair enough. 'Need a lift?'

'No, thank you. I mean to be fashionably late.'

'Do you expect me to be shackled to you all evening?' Jaz demanded.

He stiffened. Yes, dammit!

He rolled his shoulders. No, dammit.

So much for relaxation. 'We arrive together. We leave together.

We eat together. First dance and last dance.' He rattled each item off. They were non-negotiable as far as he was concerned. 'Fair enough?' he barked at her. They'd settle this before they left.

She didn't bat an eye. 'Fair enough,' she agreed.

The pulse at the base of his throat started to slow. He found he could breathe again. He meant to negotiate more than two dances out of her, come hell or high water. He meant to hold her in his arms, enjoy the feel of her, safe in the knowledge that nothing could happen in such a public place.

He turned to find Gwen staring at him with narrowed eyes. He gulped. 'I…er…want her to schmooze,' he tried to explain.

'I just bet you do,' she returned with evil knowingness.

'I…' He couldn't think of a damn thing to say.

Jaz jumped in. 'Did you know that Connor is planning to challenge Gordon Sears for the town councillor position at the next election?'

Gwen's jaw dropped. 'Are you serious? But you're not some power-hungry nob.'

'No, he's not.' Satisfaction threaded through Jaz's voice. 'Which should make him the perfect candidate, don't you think?'

He stood a little straighter at her praise, pushed his shoulders back.

'It at least makes him better than Gordon Sears, but enough of that.' Gwen dismissed the subject with a wave of her hand. 'Make Jaz's day and tell her the move is complete.'

'It's all done.' His men had moved Jaz's things out of his garage and into her flat today. He hadn't helped move those things. Whenever he'd driven into the garage, walked through the garage, walked past the garage, and saw her things there, he'd had an insane urge to go through them to try and discover a clue as to how she'd spent the last eight years. He hadn't. He wouldn't. But he'd put himself out of temptation's way today and had taken Mel for a hot chocolate and another skyway ride instead. 'You can move in and start unpacking as early as tomorrow if you want.'

When he'd driven the van into the garage this afternoon and found all her things gone, it had left a hole inside him as big as the Jamison Valley. Why?

Because you're an idiot, that's why. Because you still want her.

He ground his teeth together. He'd made a lot of mistakes in the last eight years, but he wasn't making that one. Not again. He would not kiss Jaz. He would not make love to Jaz. He would not get involved with Jaz.

Never again.

He had to think of Mel. His daughter already adored Jaz more than he thought wise. He didn't want Mel thinking of Jaz as anything other than a friend.

It would be hard enough for Mel to cope with Jaz leaving in twelve months' time, let alone…

He ran a finger around the inside of his collar again. Let alone anything more. End of story.

'I'll move into the flat on Monday,' he heard Jaz tell Gwen. 'I'm hoping business will be brisk in the bookshop tomorrow.'

She was working tomorrow? They'd better not make it a late night then. His jaw tightened. Not that he'd intended on making it a late night.

He tried to get his brain onto business and away from the personal. 'How are the new staff members working out?' She'd spent the last four days training staff the recruitment agency in Katoomba had sent her.

'So well that I'm planning on taking Monday and Tuesday off to unpack and set the flat up properly. I'll only be a shout away if needed.'

'Good. It's about time you stopped working so hard and took a couple of days off. If you're not careful you'll make yourself ill.'

Her eyes widened and he thrust his hands in his pockets with a scowl. That comment had been way too personal. He started to spell *businesslike* out in his mind again.

Speculation fired to life in Gwen's face. She raised an

eyebrow at Jaz. Jaz pressed her lips together and gave one tight shake of her head. Connor adjusted his tie. It seemed a whole lot tighter now than it had when he'd left home.

Gwen laughed. 'You two give off as much heat as you ever did.'

His collar tightened until he thought he'd choke. Jaz's eyes all but started from her head.

Jaz swung to him. 'Speaking of heat…'

He wondered if he'd ever breathe again.

'…is the town hall still heated? Or should I change into something warmer? Something with longer sleeves?'

'Don't change!' The words burst out of him with revealing rapidity.

He coughed and quickly overrode Gwen's triumphant 'Aha!'

He rapped out, 'It gets uncomfortably warm in the town hall. You'll be grateful for those short sleeves once the dancing starts.'

'Okay.' She gazed at him expectantly for a moment, then finally sighed. 'I'll get my handbag and wrap and then we can leave.'

The town hall was festooned with ribbons and pine cones, with fragrant boughs of eucalyptus. Beneath it all, Connor could smell the tantalising scent of wattle. He and Jaz paused as they crossed the threshold, and Connor had to bite back a grin when one section of the hall—Gordon Sears and his set—broke off their conversation around a table of hors d'oeuvres to turn and stare.

Actually…gaped summed it up more accurately.

Beside him, Jaz stiffened and he drew her hand into the crook of his arm, folded his hand over it and tried to convey to her that she wasn't alone. He hadn't brought her here to feed her to the lions. Her hand trembled beneath his, but she lifted her chin and planted a smile on her face, held herself tall and erect. That simple act of courage warmed him, made him stand taller and prouder too.

'I think it's safe to say that we've given them something to talk about for the rest of the night,' she quipped.

He released her hand to seize two glasses of champagne from the tray of a passing waiter and handed her one. 'Whereas we won't spare them another thought for the rest of the evening.'

She touched her glass to his. 'I'll drink to that.'

Her hair framed her face in a feathery style that highlighted high cheekbones and long-lashed eyes. He wanted to reach out and touch that hair, to run his fingers through it, cup a hand around the back of her head and draw her in close to—

He snapped upright, glanced around the room.

'Who should we schmooze with first?' she asked.

'This way.' With his hand in the small of her back, he turned her towards a knot of people on the opposite side of the room and tried to ignore the way the heat from her body branded his fingertips as it seeped through the thin material of her dress. With half a growl, he dragged his gaze from the seductive sway of her hips. That was when he saw Sam Hancock.

Sam Hancock without a date!

Sam and his sister hadn't sold the family home when their father had died, although neither one of them lived in Clara Falls now. They used the house as a weekender. Obviously Sam had decided to grace Clara Falls with his presence this particular weekend.

'Connor?'

Jaz's soft query drew him back, her blue-green eyes fathomless.

'I just saw your old friend Sam Hancock.' The observation didn't come out anywhere near as casual as he meant it to.

She stared at him. 'Did you want to go over and say hello?'

She'd promised to leave with him at the end of the night. He held fast to that. He tried to relax his hold on his champagne flute. She didn't crane her neck over his shoulder to catch a glimpse of Sam. She didn't push her glass of champagne into his hand and rush off to embrace her former lover. The tightness in his chest eased a fraction.

Which sent warning bells clanging through him. He didn't

want Jaz for himself, but he didn't want other men having her either?

Or was it just Sam Hancock?

He tested the theory, tried to imagine Jaz with some other man in the room—any man. His teeth ground together. No, it wasn't just Sam Hancock.

Charming. He was a dog in the manger.

Only…he did want her for himself, didn't he?

'Connor!'

He snapped to.

'I thought we were supposed to be schmoozing. Stop glaring around the room like that. You won't win any votes with that look on your face.'

He laughed. He didn't mean to, but her words—the scolding—the warmth deep down in her eyes eased his tension. 'Come and meet the Barries.' He'd enjoy the night for what it was and nothing more.

Connor found that he did enjoy the evening. Jaz conversed easily with everyone he introduced her to. The Jaz of old hadn't had that kind of confidence or social poise. The Jaz of old would've held back and spent most of the night hiding behind him. The Jaz of old had been nothing more than a girl. This Jaz—the here and now version—was a strong, confident woman. Something told him she'd earned that self-possession.

It made her ten times more potent.

She ate dinner at the table beside him. They danced the first dance… and the second… and Connor almost breathed a sigh of relief when she excused herself to go and powder her nose. He needed oxygen—big time.

It didn't stop him from watching her as she made a circuit around the room, though. Along the way, people stopped her. Here and there, she stopped of her own accord. Then she stopped by Sam Hancock, who was sitting on his own, and Connor gripped a handful of linen tablecloth. Sam leapt to his feet and said something that made her laugh. She said something back that made him laugh. Then she kept walking.

She kept walking.

He released the tablecloth. If he hadn't been sitting he'd have fallen.

It hit him then—Jaz hadn't flirted with a single man here tonight. Frieda would've flirted with every man in the room. He saw the defence behind that tactic now too—by flirting with every man present, Frieda had managed to keep them all at arm's length. About the only man she hadn't flirted with was Gordon Sears.

His heart started to burn. Jaz was not made in the same mould as her mother. Had he got it wrong eight years ago?

He remembered the sight of her in Sam Hancock's arms, the words she'd uttered that had damned her. They still proved her guilt, her infidelity.

But, suddenly, he found he wasn't quite so sure of anything.

Jaz returned from the powder room to take her seat at the table beside Connor again. All the other couples from their table were dancing. She gulped. She prayed Connor wouldn't ask her to dance again. She wasn't sure how much more of that she could take, especially now they'd dimmed the lights.

'Enjoying yourself?'

'Yes.' And she meant it. 'It's been lovely meeting up with people again.'

He set a glass of punch down in front of her. 'Non-alcoholic,' he said before she could ask. 'I know you're working tomorrow.'

'Thank you.'

She didn't reach out for the drink because her fingers had gone suddenly boneless. He looked so sure and…male in his dinner suit. His body had grown harder in the eight years she'd been away. His shoulders had become broader, his thighs more powerful. And he still created an ache of need deep down inside her like he'd always done.

She hoped he wouldn't push the stay-in-Clara-Falls-for-ever-and-make-it-your-home thing again. She couldn't stay for ever in the same town as Connor Reed. It just wouldn't work.

One corner of his mouth kinked up but it didn't warm his eyes. 'You've schmoozed beautifully.'

She raised her eyes at the edge in his voice. 'Is that supposed to be a compliment?' she asked warily.

He frowned. 'Yes.'

'Sorry.' She hadn't meant to misinterpret his mood. 'I am having fun, but this really isn't my favourite kind of do.'

'What is?'

'Beer and pizza nights.' She sighed in longing. A beer and pizza night with a bunch of her friends would go down a treat at the moment.

Connor grinned and this time the gold flecks in his eyes came out to play. 'Well, there's not a soul in this room who'd sense you'd rather be anywhere else this evening. You've charmed everyone you've met.'

She smiled at that. 'Wonders will never cease, huh? The rebel Goth girl developing a few social graces after all.'

'It's quite a change, Jaz, even you have to admit that. Where did you go when you decided not to come back to Clara Falls? What did you do? How did you manage the…transformation?'

Jaz realised she'd been waiting for him to ask that question all night. 'After I left my aunt's I went to the airport, directly to the airport, I didn't pass go and I didn't collect two hundred dollars.'

He stared at her. Jaz shrugged. 'I went to America.'

He leant forward. 'Why America?'

She'd wanted to run as far away as possible. She'd wanted to start over in a place that didn't know her. And she'd needed to make a grand gesture. 'Would you believe me if I said—because I was young and stupid?'

He smiled. 'Young, yes, but never stupid.'

He was wrong about that. 'I strode into the airport and

decided I was going to Europe or America. The travel agent must've thought me mad…or a criminal. I just asked for the first flight out. And that's how I ended up in LA with next to no money, no job and nowhere to stay. Believe me, that makes a girl start thinking on her feet pretty fast.'

'What did you do?'

'Rented a dingy hotel room for a week, bought a sketch pad and charcoals and spent the week drawing portraits of tourists on the beach and charging them five dollars a pop. That's where Carroll Carson found me. He's *the* big-name tattoo artist on the west coast.' She shrugged. 'He took me under his wing, offered me an apprenticeship. I was lucky.'

She glanced across at him and something inside her shifted. Perhaps Mrs Lavender had been right and Jaz had done the right thing leaving Clara Falls all those years ago. If she hadn't left, she'd have spent her life living in Connor's shadow, grateful to him for loving a misfit like her.

She wasn't a misfit. She'd earned her place in the world. She didn't need any man to make that right.

'Faye was a one-night stand.'

The admission shot out of Connor like bullets from a gun, and with as much impact. All Jaz could do was stare. She wanted to tell him it wasn't any of her business.

'A one-night stand?' Her voice came out hoarse and raspy.

He scratched a hand back through his hair. 'Faye was the one who told me about you and Sam Hancock.'

Her jaw dropped. Surely Faye hadn't thought—

'You'd left. We both missed you like the blazes. We drank too much and…'

He trailed off with a shrug. She was glad he didn't go into details.

'The next day I told her that it had been a mistake. That it couldn't happen again.'

Jaz stared at him, shook her head, tried to comprehend what he was telling her. 'How did she take that?'

'Not well.'

Had Faye been in love with Connor all along? The thought made her feel suddenly ill. 'Why are you telling me this?' She found herself on her feet, shaking with…she wasn't sure what— more regrets? She didn't have room for any more of those.

Connor stood too. 'I just wanted you to know the truth, that's all.'

The gold sparks in Connor's eyes, their concern, reached out and wrapped her in their warmth. The same way his arms had wrapped around her when they'd danced. It had near sent her pulse sky-rocketing off the charts.

She pulled back. There was no future for her and Connor. There was no point wondering what it would be like to rest her head against his shoulder or to nuzzle her face against his neck, to slip her hand beneath his shirt and trace the contours of muscle and sinew honed by hard physical labour.

There might not be any point to it, but she couldn't seem to stop imagining it.

'Hey, guys, having fun?'

Gwen, cheeks flushed from dancing, bore down on them.

'Absolutely,' Jaz managed.

'You bet,' Connor said. 'You look as if you're slaying them in the aisles.'

Jaz ground her teeth together.

'Are you drinking that?' Gwen pointed to the glass of punch. Jaz handed it to her. 'Help yourself.'

'Thanks.' She drained it dry. 'Ooh, look, there's Tim Wilder. I'll catch you both later.'

'You bet. Go knock him dead.'

That was Connor again.

'Are you okay?' he asked when he turned back to Jaz.

She slammed her hands to her hips. Connor backed up a step. 'You have that itching for a fight look plastered all over your face. What have I done this time?'

'It's what you haven't done. Or, more precisely, what you

haven't said. Is there something wrong with my appearance?' she demanded.

He shoved his hands in his pockets. 'No.' He shifted his feet. 'Why?'

'Because you've told every woman you've met this evening how lovely or stunning or wonderful she looks. Every woman, that is, except me!'

A grin spread across his face, slow and sure. His shoulders lost their tightness. He moved in closer, crowding her with his heat, his scent…their history. He angled his body towards hers in a blatant invitation she wanted to accept.

'Does my opinion matter so much to you, Jaz?'

'No, of course not,' she snapped, angry with herself. 'Put it down to a moment of feminine insecurity.'

She tried to move past him but his arm snaked out and caught her around the waist, drew her back against his heat and his hardness. With agonising slowness and thoroughness, he splayed his hand across her stomach. Low down across her stomach. She bit back a whimper. If he moved that hand, if he moved so much as his little finger, she'd melt in his arms where she stood.

'You don't have any reason whatsoever for insecurity, Jazmin.'

His breath touched her ear. She closed her eyes. He'd only ever called her Jazmin when they'd made love. And in the eight long years since she'd left here, she'd never had another lover. Not one. Trembling shivers that started at her knees and moved upwards shook her body, betraying her need.

'But if I start telling you how sexy you look in that dress, how wearing your hair like that highlights your eyes and how the gloss on your lips makes my mouth water…then that might lead to me telling you how I want to tear that dress from your body and make love to you all night long—fast and frantic the first time, slow and sensual the second time, watching every nuance in your face the third time.'

She couldn't find her voice. Her breath came in short shallow gulps.

'But, given the circumstances, that might not be wise.'

No, not wise at all.

He pulled her more firmly against him until she couldn't mistake the hardness pressing against the small of her back. 'I burn for you as much as I ever did, Jazmin.'

His teeth grazed her ear. She moaned.

'I can feel that same need burning in you. I can feel your body trembling for me. I want to take you home and make love to you. Now. Just say the word,' he murmured against her ear, 'and we're out of here. Say it!' he ordered.

Yes! To spend a glorious night of pleasure and freedom in Connor's arms. Yes! To touch him as her fingers and lips burned to do, to scale the heights with him and...

No.

Her heart dropped. She gulped. She peeled his fingers from her stomach, one by one, and stepped away. 'And what happens tomorrow, Connor?' She turned to face him. 'And the day after that?' Did he think they could just pick up where they'd left off?

The flush of desire in his eyes didn't abate. 'We—'

'What happens the next time you find me with another man in a situation you can't account for? Are you going to fly off the handle and accuse me of cheating on you again?'

His head snapped back.

'You didn't trust me then and you don't trust me now.' More importantly, she didn't trust herself. Who would she hurt the next time he broke her heart?

There wouldn't be a next time!

She had no intention of losing her heart to him ever again. No man was worth that kind of pain. 'If you'll excuse me, I'm in serious need of a glass of punch.'

She turned and stalked off in the direction of the refreshments table and she didn't wait to see if he followed. From the evidence she'd seen, he'd need a moment to himself.

She helped herself to punch, started to raise the glass to her lips, when Gordon Sears bore down on her.

'I've been looking for you everywhere, Jaz.'

She loathed his fake jovial tone, the smirk on his face. She ignored the headache pounding at her temples to inject a false brightness of her own. 'Why's that, Mr S? Did you want to ask me to dance?'

'No, just wanted to give you advance warning that I'll be serving papers on your solicitor come Monday morning.'

Her stomach started to churn. 'What kind of papers?'

'No doubt you're aware that I lent your mother fifty thousand dollars?'

Punch sloshed over the side of her glass.

Satisfaction settled over his face. 'No?' he said. 'That was remiss of her.'

'I don't believe you,' she whispered. Why would Frieda borrow money from this man?

'She needed it to buy the bookshop.' He rubbed his hands together, his smile widening. 'And now I'm calling in that debt. Pay up within seven days or the bookshop is mine.'

Fifty thousand dollars! She didn't have that kind of money. He had to be bluffing.

He had to be bluffing!

Oh, Mum. Why? To lure me back to Clara Falls? I wasn't worth it.

'Is there a problem?' Connor demanded, striding up and placing himself between Jaz and Mr Sears.

Mr Sears threw his head back and laughed. 'Not for much longer.' With that, he swaggered off.

Connor's brows drew down low over his eyes. 'What was that all about?'

'Just Mr Sears trying to cause trouble as usual.' But her voice shook.

His eyes narrowed. 'Has he succeeded?'

She lifted her chin, forced her shoulders back. 'Of course not.' She glared at him. 'But why couldn't this have just been a beer and pizza night, huh?' She could do with a fat-laden pepperoni pizza right now, washed down with an ice-cold beer. It might help her think.

It might help her sleep.

Connor frowned. 'Are you feeling okay, Jaz?'

'I'm perfect,' she snapped.

He stared down at her for a long moment. 'You look beat. Are you ready to leave?'

She gave a fervent nod. 'Yes, please.'

CHAPTER NINE

JAZ stood outside the door of her upstairs flat and turned the key over and over in her hand. She tried to regulate her breathing, her heart rate.

With an impatient movement, she shoved the key in the lock, but she didn't turn it. She drew back again to twist her hands together. *Jeez Louise!*

She'd made excuses whenever Connor had asked her if she wanted to inspect the flat. Same with the carpet-layers. And the men who'd fitted the blinds and light-fittings. She couldn't make any more excuses. What on earth would she say to Gwen if she delayed moving into the flat any longer—*I don't want to enter the place where my mother lost all of her hope?*

It wouldn't do.

But she still didn't move forward to open the door.

'Hello, Jaz.'

She jumped and swung around, clutching her heart. 'Connor!' She gulped. 'I…um…didn't hear you.'

He stood two steps below the landing. Wooden steps. *Rickety* wooden steps. She had a feeling that she really ought to have heard him.

He didn't point out that his work boots must've made plenty of noise. He stared at the closed door and then at her. 'Are you okay?'

'Of course I am.'

'Then what are you doing?'

'I was just about to go into the flat, that's all.'

In one hand he held a large parcel wrapped in brown paper. She wondered what it was. She wondered what he could be doing here with it. She brightened. Perhaps he hadn't finished work on the flat after all and still had one or two things to install? It'd give her a legitimate excuse to race back to Gwen's B&B.

'Housewarming gift,' he explained, gesturing to it.

Darn!

Then she remembered her manners. 'That's nice of you, Connor. But you certainly didn't have to go to any trouble.'

'No trouble.'

He glanced at the door again, then back at her. 'Besides, I wanted to.'

For a moment his eyes burned and she recalled with more clarity than she could've thought possible the feel of his hand on her abdomen when it had rested there on Saturday night, his breath against her neck.

'Are you going to open the door?'

She gulped and swung back to the door. 'Yes, of course I am.' But she didn't reach out and unlock it.

Connor moved up the final two steps with a grace she'd have appreciated all the more if her heart hadn't tried to dash itself against her ribs.

'I knew there was a problem when you kept making excuses not to inspect the flat.'

'No problem. I just trusted your workmanship. That's all.'

'Your mother didn't die inside there, you know, Jaz.'

'I know that!' Her mother had died later at the hospital. 'Like I said, there's no problem.'

He ignored that. 'Okay, the way I see it, I can either pick you up and physically carry you inside…'

Good Lord, no. Bad, bad idea. She didn't want him touching her.

Yes, you do, a little voice whispered through her.

Fine, then. She didn't want what it might lead to.

Are you so sure?

She ignored that. 'Or?'

'Or I can watch your back while you go first.'

That didn't fill her with a great deal of enthusiasm either.

'Or I can go first.'

She met the amber and gold flecks in his eyes. He hadn't stated the obvious—that he could leave. She should tell him to go.

'If I go first I can give you the grand tour. I can point out the work the guys and I have done. You can ooh and ahh over all the improvements.'

She moistened her lips, then nodded. 'I'd…um…appreciate that.'

'I want you to be the one to unlock the door, Jaz.'

She gulped again. His eyes held hers—steady…patient. She didn't glance at the door again. She kept her gaze on his face and soaked up all his warmth and strength. With fingers that shook, she reached out and unlocked the door.

Connor smiled. She wished she could smile back, but she couldn't. He moved past her, gathered her hand inside his and led her into the flat.

'As you can see, the flat is a gun-barrel affair.'

His matter-of-fact tone soothed her.

'This door is the only entrance and exit to the flat. So if a fire ever starts down this end and you're at the other end, you'll need to climb out the front windows onto the shop awning and swing down to the street from there.'

'Just call me Tarzan,' she muttered.

He grinned and, although she couldn't grin back, it eased some of the tightness in her chest.

He gestured to the left. 'We ripped the old bathroom out and replaced it.'

She stuck her head around the door—black and white tiles. 'Nice.'

'This is the kitchen. Another rip-out-and-replace job.'

The hallway opened out into a neat kitchen. Connor and his men had done a nice job. She ran her free hand across a kitchen cupboard, a countertop. Her other hand felt warm and secure in Connor's.

'Very nice,' she managed.

They didn't stop to study it any further. Connor tugged her up the three steps that led into the enormous combined dining and living area, towed her into the centre of the room and then dropped her hand. Jaz turned on the spot. Even with all her boxes piled up in here, she could make out that the proportions of the room were generous.

Perfect for dinner parties.

And beer and pizza evenings.

Some more of that soul-sickening tension eased out of her.

'Why don't you go explore further?'

He smiled that steady, patient smile and his strength arced across the space between them to flood her. With a nod, she followed a short passageway to the two bedrooms—a small one on the left and a large bright one at the front that held her bed, wardrobe and dressing table. Light poured in at two large windows. She leant on the nearest windowsill and stared out at the vista spread before her—a glorious view of Clara Falls' main street, framed by the mountains in the background.

Her mother had lived in this flat without proper heating, without a working gas stove and with rotting floorboards in one section of the living room because of a leak in the roof, not to mention the wood rot in the kitchen and bathroom. Yet…

Jaz's lips curved up. Her mother would've thought that a small price to pay for this view.

Frieda would also have loved the wood-panelled walls and pressed tin ceilings. She'd have been happy here.

Relief hit Jaz then—lovely, glorious relief. She dropped to her knees by the window, lifted her face to the sun and murmured a prayer of thanks. She hadn't come upstairs once the last two weeks, afraid that the despair that must've enveloped her mother would still hang heavy and grim in these rooms. She'd expected it to taunt her, berate her…sap her of her energy and her determination.

She'd welcomed every delay—first by the carpet layers, then by the firm who'd measured the flat for blinds and curtains, and then the gas board. Even this morning—after she'd rung Richard to warn him of Mr Sears's threats—she'd hung around and dithered in the shop until her staff had shooed her out with promises to call her if she was needed.

But the air didn't press down on her with suffocating heaviness, punishing her for not coming home sooner. It didn't silently and darkly berate her for abandoning her mother. She opened her eyes. The mid-morning sunlight twinkled in at the windows and the flat smelt fresh and clean and full of promise.

She pushed herself to her feet and glanced out of the window at Mr Sears's 'baked-fresh-daily' country bakery and resolve settled over her shoulders.

She had boxes to unpack.

'Connor?'

He hadn't followed her into the bedroom, and the click of the front door told her he'd just left.

She stared down the empty corridor and her heart burned. He'd sensed the demons that had overtaken her. He'd helped her face them…and then he'd left? Just like that? He hadn't let her thank him.

The housewarming gift!

She raced back out to the living room and tugged off the brown paper wrapping. She sat back on her heels and stared. Her throat thickened and she had to swallow.

He'd given her the handmade wine rack she'd admired so much that day in his garage.

With a hand that shook, she reached out and ran a finger across the smooth wood. 'Thank you,' she whispered into the silence.

* * *

Jaz hadn't thought to check if the electricity had been connected to the flat until shadows started to lengthen around her. She glared at the light switch on the wall, but she didn't reach out to switch it on and see. She glared around the kitchen. She'd made progress today—good progress.

For all the good it would do her.

Richard had called her an hour ago—Mr Sears's claim was legitimate. Jaz had to find fifty thousand dollars in the next seven days or lose the bookshop.

A knock sounded on the door and Jaz raced to answer it, welcoming the interruption. 'Mrs Lavender! What are you doing here? Come in.'

Mrs Lavender tsk-tsked. 'You'll ruin your eyesight, Jazmin Harper!' She moved past Jaz, flicked on the light and bathed the kitchen in a warm glow. 'That's better. Now, I can't stay. I just wanted to bring you up some supplies.'

The older woman's thoughtfulness touched her. 'You didn't need to go to any trouble.'

'No trouble, dear. It's just some coffee, a carton of milk and a loaf of bread. Oh, and some eggs,' she said, pulling the items out of a muslin bag. 'Now, don't work too late and don't forget to eat.'

'I won't,' Jaz promised. On impulse, she reached out and hugged the older woman. 'Thank you.'

She saw Mrs Lavender out, then came back in and stared up at the kitchen light sending out its golden glow.

'It's a good sign,' she announced to a pile of empty boxes in the corner. 'It's a good sign,' she said to the jug, filling it. She needed all the good signs she could get.

'Oh, stop talking to yourself and go make your bed!'

She flicked on every light as she went. She made her bed, straightened the bedside tables. She hunted out her bedside clock, a couple of paperbacks and a framed photograph of Frieda.

Now it looked as if someone lived here.

Hands on hips, she surveyed the room and decided the dressing table would look better on the opposite wall. She set her shoulder against it, out-of-all-proportion grateful for castor wheels. The dressing table moved an inch, then stuck fast. She tried hauling it towards her instead. Same result. With a grunt she managed to pull it out from the wall, and reached behind to investigate.

'Darn.' A panel of wood was wedged between wall and dressing table. It must've fallen off the wall. Biting back a very rude word, she pulled it out and set it aside, shoved her dressing table into its new location with more speed than grace, then turned to assess the damage.

Connor had said the bedrooms in the flat were structurally sound. That all they'd need was a coat of paint...and new carpet...and new blinds and curtains. 'What do you call this?' she grumbled. Then remembered she wasn't supposed to be talking to herself.

She tried to fit the panel back to the wall.

She didn't try biting back that very rude word when the panel fell off the wall again.

She seized it in both hands and held it like a club. She could tattoo big, burly men without batting an eyelash. She could do a pretty good Carly Simon rendition on karaoke nights, but home maintenance?

Very carefully she set the panel of wood on the floor, hauled in a deep breath and massaged her temples. For reasons of personal pride, it had become important to fix this slim panel of wood back to the wall. She needed to work out how piece A fitted into piece B. It took her all of five seconds to realise she'd need a torch.

'At least I have one of those.'

She rushed out to the living room to rifle through boxes, and forgot to berate herself for talking out loud. 'Aha!' She held the torch aloft in triumph. 'Yes!' The battery even worked.

She raced back to the bedroom and studied the piece of wood panelling thoroughly, and then the wall. What she needed to do was—

Something glittered in the gap in the wall. Jaz squinted, adjusted the torch. An old Christmas shortbread tin?

She hesitated for only a moment before pushing her hand through the hole. 'But if anything black and hairy so much as touches me…'

Her fingers closed around the tin and she drew it out. She set it on the floor and stared at it. 'Wouldn't I love to find fifty thousand dollars inside you,' she murmured.

She reached out, ran her fingers across the tin's lid—remarkably dust-free. She shone her torch into the wall cavity—*not* remarkably dust-free.

She clambered to her feet, tucked the tin under her arm and went to make herself a cup of coffee.

She sipped her coffee on the steps between the kitchen and living room and surveyed the tin. 'If this were a novel, I really would find fifty thousand dollars in you, you know? And, as we are sitting above a bookshop…' She lifted a hand, then let it fall. 'All I'm trying to say is, if you'd like to come to the party I don't have any complaints.'

She set her mug down and pulled the tin towards her. 'With my luck it'll be a bomb,' she grumbled.

She hauled the lid off.

She stared.

And then she smiled.

Letters. Letters addressed to Frieda Harper, tied in pink ribbon and scented with rose petals. 'Oh, Mum—' she sighed '—who'd have guessed you had such a romantic streak?'

She untied the ribbon, lifted the first letter from the pile, eased it out of its envelope and unfolded it.

My beloved Frieda.

Oh, how beautiful. Jaz's hand went to her chest. She turned the letter over, searching for the signature, the name of her mother's admirer, and—

No!

She abandoned the letter to tear open the next one…and the

one after that…until she'd checked them all. They all bore the same signature.

She pinched herself. She started to laugh. She leapt to her feet and danced around the room. 'We've saved the bookshop, Mum!'

The tin didn't hold fifty thousand dollars. It held love letters addressed to her mother from Gordon Sears.

Gordon Sears!

If the contents of these letters became public, his credibility would be ruined in Clara Falls for ever.

She swept the letters and the tin up, along with her still-warm cup of coffee, and raced out of the flat and downstairs to the bookshop to address the portrait of Frieda on the wall. The one she hadn't finished yet. Couldn't finish.

That didn't stop her talking to it. 'Look!' She held the letters up for Frieda to see. 'I don't know if you meant for me to find these, Mum, but you didn't destroy them so…' She hauled in a breath and tried to contain her excitement. 'They couldn't have come at a better time. I can save the bookshop with these.'

For the first time she found she could smile back at the laughing eyes in Frieda's portrait.

She set her mug on the floor, opened the tin and started reading the letters out loud to her mother. 'I would've only been eleven when you received this one.'

But, as she continued to read, her elation started to fade. 'Oh, Mum…' She finished reading the third letter, folded it and slipped it back into its envelope. She settled herself on the floor beneath her mother's portrait. 'He must've loved you so very much.'

Her triumph turned to pity then, and compassion. Very slowly she eased the tin's lid back into place, pulled it up to her chest and hugged it.

That was how Connor found her half an hour later.

'Am I interrupting anything?'

'No.' She eased the tin back down to her lap.

'I saw the light on and it reminded me that I hadn't returned your key.'

She studied his face as he settled on the floor beside her. She snorted her disbelief at his excuse. 'Richard's spoken to you, hasn't he? Isn't there such a thing as a professional code of privacy in this town?'

'All he said was that you might need a friend this evening, nothing else.'

'Oh.'

'You haven't finished Frieda's portrait yet.'

She couldn't. She didn't know why, but she just couldn't. 'I've been busy.'

She had a feeling he saw through the lie.

'Want to tell me what's going on?'

'Why not?' She didn't bother playing dumb. 'It'll be common knowledge around town soon enough.' She leant her head against the wall. 'My mother borrowed fifty thousand dollars from Gordon Sears. He's calling the debt in.'

'Fifty thousand dollars!' Connor shot forward. 'Are you serious?'

She nodded. 'And no,' she added, answering the next question in his eyes, 'I don't have access to that kind of money. But I do have an appointment with the bank manager first thing tomorrow.'

She dragged a hand down her face. She didn't want to think what would happen if the bank refused her the loan.

Sympathy and concern blazed from Connor's eyes. It bathed her in a warmth she hadn't expected. If felt nice having him sit here on the floor beside her like this—comforting. Perhaps Richard was right and she did need a friend. Maybe, given enough time—and with a concerted effort on her part to ignore the attraction that simmered through her whenever she saw him—she and Connor could be friends.

'Thank you for stopping by and making sure I was okay. I do appreciate it.' Perhaps they were friends already?

'You're welcome.'

She met his eyes. Their gold sparks flashed and glittered and tension coiled through her—that tight, gut-busting yearning she needed to find a way to control. Finally, as if he too could no longer bear it, his gaze dropped to the tin in her lap and she could breathe again.

He nodded towards it. 'What have you got there?'

Without a word, she passed the tin across to him, watched the expressions that chased themselves across his face as he opened it and read the top letter.

'Bloody hell, Jaz! Do you know what this means?' He held the letter up in his long work-roughened fingers, leaning forward in his excitement. 'This is your bargaining chip. Show these to Gordon Sears and he will definitely come to some agreement with you about paying back the loan. They're pure gold!'

'Yes.'

He stilled, studied her face. 'You're not going to use them, are you?'

'No.'

'But…'

She sympathised with the way the air left his lungs, the way he sagged back against the wall to stare at her as if he couldn't possibly have heard her properly.

'I'm not going to use these letters to blackmail Mr Sears.' She couldn't use them.

She tried to haul her mind back from thoughts of dragging Connor's mouth down to hers and kissing him until neither one of them could think straight. Which would be a whole lot easier to do if the scent of autumn hadn't settled all around her, making her yearn for the impossible.

'Why not?'

She took a letter from the tin. *'My beloved Frieda,'* she read. *'All my love…forever yours.'* She dropped it back into the tin. The action sent his scent swirling around her all the more. She breathed it in. She couldn't do anything else. 'To use that as blackmail would be to desecrate something very beautiful. I won't do it.'

She gestured to the unfinished portrait above them. 'My

mother wouldn't want me to do it.' She wanted to make Frieda proud of her, not ashamed.

Connor stared at her for a long time and those beautiful broad shoulders of his bowed as if a sudden weight had dropped onto them. His mouth tightened, the lines around it and his eyes became deeper and more pronounced. His skin lost its colour. His autumn eyes turned as bleak as winter.

Her heart thudded in sudden fear. 'Connor?'

'You didn't cheat on me eight years ago, did you, Jaz? I got it wrong. I got it all wrong.'

Her skin went cold, then hot. She hunched her knees up towards her chest and wrapped her arms around them. 'No, I didn't cheat on you.'

She hadn't thought he could go any paler. She'd been wrong. She wanted to reach out a hand and offer him some kind of comfort but she was too afraid to. She'd always known it would rock him to his foundations if he ever discovered the truth. She recognised the regret, the guilt, the sorrow that stretched through his eyes. Recognised too the self-condemnation, the belief in the inadequacy of any apology he tried to offer now.

She should've stayed eight years ago. She should've stayed and fought for him.

She couldn't change the past but...

'What time is it?'

He glanced at his watch, stared at it for an eternity, then shook himself. 'It's only half past six.'

'Is your car out the back?'

He nodded.

'C'mon then.' She rose. 'There's something I want to show you.'

He followed her outside, waited for her to lock the bookshop, then led her to his car. 'Where to?' he asked, starting the engine.

'Sam Hancock's.'

He swung to face her but he didn't say anything. Did he think she meant to punish him? He set his shoulders, his mouth a grim line and she could almost see a mantle of resolve settle over him as he started the car. He intended to endure whatever she threw at him.

Oh, Connor. I don't want to hurt you any more. I want you to understand and find peace, that's all.

They didn't speak as he drove the short distance to Sam's house. Nor did they speak as she led the way to the front door. Sam had told her on Saturday night that he was here for the next week.

'Hi, Sam,' she said when he answered the door. 'You told me the other night that I was welcome to come around and view my handiwork if I wanted. Is now a convenient time?'

'Absolutely.' With a smile, he ushered them into the house and led them through to the main bedroom, gestured to the life-size painting on the wall. 'I'll leave you to it. Yell if you need anything.'

Jaz murmured her thanks but barely managed to drag her gaze away from Connor as he studied the picture she'd painted of Lenore Hancock eight years ago. 'This is Sam's mother,' she said because she had to say something.

'Yes.' He moved closer to it to study it more carefully.

'This is where I first understood the power of my talent.'

He turned to meet her gaze and she shrugged. 'I hadn't fully comprehended the effect something like this could have. It frightened me.'

He gestured to the wall too, but he didn't glance back at the picture. His eyes remained glued to her face. 'How did this come about?'

'Sam's dad developed dementia and started walking the streets at all times of the day and night searching for Lenore. She'd died a couple of years before him, you see.'

'So you drew her on the wall for him?'

'Yes.'

'Why didn't you tell me?'

'Because Sam and his sister asked me to keep it a secret.'

His hands clenched. 'Even from me?'

She wanted to reach out and wipe the anguish from his eyes. 'Sam and his sister didn't want to put their father into a nursing home, but they both had to work and the nurse who came for a few hours every day was finding him harder and harder to deal with. The fewer people who knew, the fewer people who could interfere.'

She pulled in a breath. She owed him the whole truth. 'What I felt for you, Connor…it scared me too. Some days I thought you would swallow me whole. I needed to find my own place in the world that was separate from yours.' And she'd found it in the worst way possible. 'Though it never occurred to me that you could misconstrue…'

He stepped back, his lips pressed together so tightly they almost turned blue. Her stomach turned to ash. Could he even begin to understand her insecurity back then?

He swung away to stare at the picture again. 'Did it work? Did they have to put Mr Hancock into a nursing home?'

'It worked better than any of us had dreamed.' She bit her lip, remembering the evening they'd unveiled the finished portrait to Mr Hancock. 'When he saw the picture, he pulled up a chair and started talking to her I'll never forget his first words. He said—*Lenore, I've been looking for you everywhere, love. And now I've found you.*' It had damn near broken her heart. She'd had to back out of the room and race outside.

Connor swung around as if he sensed that emotion close to the surface in her now. 'That's the same night I found you with Sam, isn't it?'

She hesitated, then nodded.

'Mr Hancock's reaction, it freaked you out, didn't it? It wore you out the same way that tattoo you did for Jeff wore you out.'

'Yes.' The word whispered out of her.

'And Sam was trying to comfort you.'

Her throat closed over. She managed a nod.

'When you said—*I loathe this thing and I love it too, but whatever I do I can't give it up*—you were talking about your ability to draw people so well, so accurately, and not about your relationship with Sam.'

Her head snapped up. 'Is that what you thought?' She stared at him in shock.

'I should have believed in you.'

Yes, he should've. 'I should have stayed and made you listen.'

Eight years ago, she'd been too afraid to stay and fight for him.

'God, Jaz, I'm sorry!' He reached out one hand towards her, but he let it drop before it could touch her. 'Is it too late to apologise?'

She smiled then. 'It's never too late to apologise.' She had to believe that.

'Then I'm sorry I jumped to conclusions eight years ago. I'm sorry I accused you of cheating on me. I'm sorry for hurting you.'

A weight lifted from her. 'Thank you.'

He reached for her then and she knew he meant to fold her in his arms and kiss her.

She wanted that. She wanted that more than she'd ever wanted anything.

She took a step back. Her heart burned. Her eyes burned. 'It's not too late for apologies, but it is too late for hope. We can't turn time back. I'm sorry, Connor, but it's too late for us.'

He stilled. He dragged a hand back through his hair, his mouth grim. 'Do you really believe that?'

The words rasped out of his throat, raw, and Jaz wanted to close her eyes and rest her head against his shoulder. She stiffened her spine and forced herself to meet his gaze. 'Yes, I do.' Because it was true.

His mouth became even grimmer. 'Does this mean we can't be friends?' she whispered. She could at least have that much, couldn't she?

The mouth didn't soften. The gold highlights in his eyes didn't sparkle. 'Is that what you want?'

'Yes.' For the life of her, though, she couldn't manage a smile.

'Friends it is.'
He didn't smile either.
'C'mon.' He took her arm. 'I'll take you home.'

CHAPTER TEN

CONNOR showed up the next day for her appointment at the bank.

'What on earth…' she started.

'Friends?' he cut in, his mouth as grim as it had been last night.

'Yes, but—'

'Then trust me.'

Something about his grimness made her nod and back down. She didn't need a knight in shining armour, but it was nice knowing Connor was on her side all the same.

She got the loan. Connor told the bank manager he'd take his business—his not inconsiderable business—elsewhere if they refused her the loan. He'd have even gone guarantor for her but she put her foot down at that. The terms of the loan would stretch her resources, the bookshop would need to make a profit—and soon—all plans for an art gallery had to go on hold… But she got the loan.

'Anything else I can help with?' Connor asked once they were standing out on the footpath again.

'Well, now, let me see…' She smiled. She wanted to see the golden highlights in his eyes sparkling. She wanted to see him smile back. 'I don't have anyone lined up to man the sausage sizzle on Saturday.'

This Saturday. The Saturday of the book fair.

The book fair that now had to do well.

Very well.

'Done. I'll be there.'

He turned and strode away. No sparkling. No smiling.

She spent the rest of the week trying to lose herself in the preparations for the book fair. She double-checked that the authors and poets lined up for the Saturday afternoon readings were still available. She double-checked that the fairy she'd hired to read stories to the children hadn't come down with the flu, and that the pirates she'd hired to face-paint said children hadn't walked the plank and disappeared.

She double-checked that the enormous barbecue she'd hired would still arrive first thing Saturday morning, and that the butcher had her order for the umpteen dozen sausages she'd estimated they'd need for the sausage sizzle.

She would not let anything go wrong.

She couldn't afford to.

She didn't double-check that Connor would still man the sausage sizzle, though.

That didn't mean she could get him out of her mind.

Alone in her flat each night, she ached to ring him.

To say what?

Just to find out if he's okay.

Oh, for heaven's sake. Get over yourself. Connor has not spent the last eight years living in the past…or fleeing from it. Of course he's okay.

His men finished work on the bookshop in double-quick time…and Connor was so okay he didn't even bother coming around to check up on it.

Gritting her teeth, she wrote a cheque and posted it.

She tried to sleep but, as usual, insomnia plagued her.

By closing time on Friday afternoon, she was so wound up she didn't know if she wanted to bounce off walls or collapse into a heap.

'You're driving your staff insane, you know that?' Mrs Lavender observed.

'I'm not meaning to.' Jaz twisted her hands together and

glanced out of the window. She was always glancing out of the window. What for? Was she hoping for a sight of Connor? She dragged her gaze back.

Mrs Lavender's eyes narrowed. 'What happened to the woman who strode down the street with purpose and determination?'

'I'm still that same woman.'

'Are you? It seems to me you spend more time hand-wringing and…and mooning, these days.'

Jaz exhaled sharply. 'I'll wear the hand-wringing, but not the mooning!'

She wasn't mooning.

Was she?

She gulped. Had she let her feelings for Connor undermine her purpose?

A pulse behind her eyes hammered in time with the heart that beat against her ribs. She could not let anyone, not even Connor—especially not Connor—distract her from making her mother's dream a reality.

She nodded slowly. The hammering eased. 'You're right.' She glanced out of the window, not looking for Connor, but towards Mr Sears's bakery. As if on cue, Connor drove past with Melly in the car. Jaz refused to follow the car's progress. She didn't speak again until the car was lost from her line of sight.

'There's something I need to do,' she said with sudden decision. She didn't want to put it off any longer.

'I'll close the shop for you.'

'Thank you.'

Jaz raced upstairs, grabbed the tin of letters. Then she set off across the road to Mr Sears's 'baked-fresh-daily' country bakery.

She didn't enter the shop with a booming, Howdy, Mr S. She waited quietly to one side until he'd served the two customers in front of her, and only when they were alone did she approach the counter.

'I found something that belongs to you.' She handed him the tin, then stepped back.

Mr Sears frowned, glowered…lifted the lid of the tin…and his face went grey. The skin around his eyes, his mouth, bagged. Some force in his shoulders left him. Jaz wondered if she should race around the counter and lead him to a chair.

'What do you want?' The words rasped out of him, old-sounding and wooden. With both hands clasped around the tin, he leant his arms against the counter. Not to get closer to her, but to support himself.

'Peace,' she whispered.

He met her gaze then. He nodded. Finally he said, 'How much?'

It took her a moment to decipher his meaning. Her head snapped back when she did. He thought she wanted money?

'Or have you already given copies to the local newspapers?'

'I am my mother's daughter, Mr Sears.' She lifted her chin. 'Did my mother ever *once* threaten you with those?'

She nodded towards the letters. He didn't say anything.

'I haven't made copies, I haven't photographed them and I haven't shown them to any gossip columnists.'

She watched the way his lips twisted in disbelief and swore she would never let love tear her up, screw up her thinking, twist her, like it had in the past. Like it was doing now to Mr Sears.

'Once upon a time you loved my mother a great deal. She kept your letters, which tells me she must've loved you too. Now that she's dead they belong to you, not to anybody else.' She took a step back from the counter. 'I did not come back to Clara Falls to make my mother ashamed of me, Mr Sears.'

She turned around and walked away, knowing he didn't believe her. For the next month…three months…perhaps for the rest of his life, Gordon Sears would pick up the local paper with the taste of fear in his mouth. He'd watch for thinly disguised snickers and people falling silent whenever he walked into a room.

Until he let go of his fear, he would find no peace.

Until she let go of her fear, neither would she.

Her feet slowed to a halt outside the bookshop's brightly lit window with its colourful display of hardbacks, the posters advertising tomorrow's book fair.

Her fear.

It wasn't the fear of the bookshop failing—though, with all her heart, she needed to make that dream a reality for her mother. No, it was the fear that a true, passionate love—like the love she and Connor had once shared—would go wrong and once again she'd become bitter and destructive, hurting, even destroying, the people she most loved.

She rested her head against the cold glass. Once she'd reconciled herself to the fact that love was closed to her—love, marriage…and children. Once she'd managed that, then perhaps she'd find peace.

Jaz was awake long before she heard the tapping on the front door of her flat at seven-thirty the next morning.

At six o'clock, and over her first cup of coffee, she'd pored over the day's programme. Even though she'd memorised it earlier in the week. Then she'd started chopping onions and buttering bread rolls for the sausage sizzle. She was counting on the smell of frying onions to swell the crowd at the book fair by at least twenty per cent. Who could resist the smell of frying onions?

And who could be tapping so discreetly on her front door, as if they were worried about disturbing her, this early in the morning?

Unless the barbecue and hotplate had arrived already.

She wondered if Connor would show up and man the sausage sizzle as he'd promised.

Of course he would. Connor always kept his promises.

She tried to push all thoughts of him out of her head as she rushed to answer the door.

'Melly!'

Melly stood there, hopping from one foot to the other as if

her small frame could hardly contain her excitement. 'Did I wake you up?'

'No, I've been up for ages and ages.'

Jaz ushered her into the flat, patted a stool at the breakfast bar and poured her a glass of orange juice. 'What are you doing here?'

Melly clutched a crisp white envelope in one hand and she held it out to Jaz now. 'I had to show you this.' She grinned. She bounced in her seat.

Jaz took the envelope and read the enclosed card, and had a feeling that her grin had grown as wide as Melly's. 'This is an invitation to Yvonne Walker's slumber party tonight!'

Melly nodded so vigorously she almost fell off her stool. Jaz swooped down and hugged her. 'Sweetheart, I'm so happy for you.'

'I knew you would be. I wanted to come over yesterday to tell you, but Daddy said you were busy.'

Did he? 'I…er…see.'

Melly bit her lip. 'Are you busy now?'

'Not too busy for you,' she returned promptly.

Melly's autumn-brown eyes grew so wide with wonder Jaz found herself blinking madly.

'Then…then can you do my hair up in a ponytail bun this afternoon? I…I want to look pretty.'

'Absolutely, and you'll knock their socks off,' Jaz promised. But…

'Daddy knows you're here now, though, doesn't he?'

Melly shook her head. 'He was sleeping and I didn't want to wake him up. He was awake most of last night.'

Jaz wondered why. Then she stiffened. Good Lord! If Connor woke and found Melly gone…

Melly bit her lip again. 'Are you cross with me?'

'No, of course not, Melly, it's just… How would you feel if you woke up and couldn't find Daddy anywhere in the house?'

'I'd be scared.'

'How do you think Daddy will feel if he wakes up and he can't find you?'

Melly's eyes went wide again. 'Will he be scared too?'

Jaz nodded gravely. 'He'll be very, very worried.'

Melly leapt down from her stool. 'Maybe he's not awake yet and if I run home really, really fast…'

Jaz prayed Connor hadn't woken yet. She grabbed her car keys. 'It'll be quicker if I drive you.'

She cast a glance around at all the preparations she'd started, then shook her head. It'd only take a minute or two to see Melly home safe. She had plenty of time before the book fair kicked off at ten.

She gulped. Lord, if Connor woke and couldn't find Melly…

'Hurry, Jaz! I don't want to worry Daddy.'

Jaz stopped trying to moderate her pace. She grabbed Melly's hand and raced for the door. She released Melly to lock the door behind them and, when she turned back, Melly had already started down the stairs. Jaz had almost caught up with her when a voice boomed out, 'Melanie Linda Reed, you are in so much trouble!'

Connor! He'd woken up.

At the sound of his voice Melly swung around and Jaz could see the child's foot start to fly out from beneath her. It would send her hurtling head first down the rest of the stairs. Jaz lunged forward to grab the back of Melly's jumper, pulling the child in close to her chest. She tried to regain her balance but couldn't quite manage it and her left arm and side crashed into the railing, taking the brunt of the impact.

She gritted her teeth at the sound of her shirt sleeve tearing. Exhaled sharply as pain ripped her arm from elbow to shoulder. Struggled to her feet again.

Connor was there in seconds, lifting Melly from her arms and checking the child for injury.

'Is she okay?' Jaz managed.

He nodded.

'We were trying to get home really fast,' Melly said with a

sob. 'Jaz said you'd be really, really worried if you woke up and couldn't find me. I'm sorry, Daddy.'

Jaz wanted to tell him to go easy on Melly, but her arm was on fire and it took all her strength to stay upright.

'We'll talk about it later, Mel, but you have to promise me you'll never do that again.'

'I promise.'

'Good. Now I want to make sure Jaz didn't hurt herself.'

Jaz gave up trying to stay upright and sat.

Connor set Melly back down and they turned to her as one.

As one, their eyes widened.

Jaz tried to smile. 'I think I scratched my arm.' She couldn't look at it. She could do other people's blood, but her own made her feel a bit wobbly.

And she knew there was blood. She could feel it.

'You're bleeding, Jaz.' Melly's eyes filled with tears. 'Lots!'

It didn't mean she wanted it confirmed.

'What was it, Connor? A rusty nail?'

He glanced at the railing above, narrowed his eyes, then nodded.

'Brilliant! So now I'll have to go and get a tetanus shot.' It was the day of the book fair. She didn't have time for tetanus shots. *Oh, Mum, I'm sorry.*

Connor kicked the railing. 'I'm going to replace this whole damn structure! It's a safety hazard.' Then he took her arm in gentle fingers and surveyed it.

Melly sat down beside Jaz and stroked her right hand. 'You saved my life,' she whispered in awe.

That made Jaz smile. She squeezed the child's hand gently. 'No, I didn't, sweetheart. I saved you from a nasty tumble, that's all.'

'I'm sorry, Jaz, but I think you're going to need more than a tetanus shot.'

She gulped. 'Stitches?'

He nodded.

'But…but I don't have time for all this today.' The book fair! 'Can't we put it off till tomorrow? Please?'

'It'll take no time at all,' he soothed as if to a frightened child. He brushed her hair back from her face. 'Mel and I will take you to the hospital in Katoomba and they'll have you fixed up within two shakes of a lamb's tail, I promise.'

He looked so strong and male. Jaz wanted to snuggle against his chest and stay there.

'Daddy is a really good hand holder, Jaz. You will hold Jaz's hand, won't you, Daddy?'

'I will,' he promised.

It reminded Jaz that she should at least look brave for Melly's sake. 'No time at all, you say?'

'That's right.' He slipped an arm around her waist. 'Come on, I'll help you to the car.'

She had no choice but to submit. *Oh, Mum, I'm sorry.*

They were at the hospital for four hours.

Four hours!

Connor wanted to roar at the staff, he wanted to tear his hair out…he wanted to take away Jaz's pain.

He paced. He called his father to come and collect Melly. He rang Mrs Lavender to tell her what had happened. He held Jaz's hand.

Until they took her away and wouldn't let him go with her.

He replayed over and over in his mind that moment when Jaz had thrown herself forward to save Mel from harm. He'd been a bloody fool to roar at Mel like that, but he'd been so darn relieved to find her…

Over and over he relived his fear of that moment when he'd thought both Mel and Jaz would fall headlong down those stairs together.

One certainty crystallised in his mind with a clarity that made his hands clench. From now on, he wanted to keep Jaz from all harm. For ever.

It wasn't too late for them. It couldn't be!

Finally Jaz reappeared. She had some colour in her cheeks again and a bandage around her upper arm. She smiled at him as if she sensed his worry and wanted to allay it. 'Right as rain again, see.' She held up a piece of paper. 'I just need to get this prescription filled and then we can go.'

The nurse accompanying Jaz folded her arms. 'And what else did the doctor say, Ms Harper?'

'I'll have something to eat when I get home, I promise.'

'You'll do no such thing.' The nurse transferred her glare to Connor. 'You will take her down to the cafeteria and you won't let her leave until she's had a sandwich and an orange juice, you hear?'

'Yes, ma'am.'

'But the book fair—'

'No arguments,' he told Jaz. They'd follow the doctor's orders. 'You've been here four hours; another twenty or so minutes won't make any difference.'

She glared at him. 'You said two shakes of a lamb's tail.' She snorted. He couldn't really blame her. When her shoulders slumped he wanted to gather her in close and hold her.

He didn't. He took her for a sandwich and an orange juice.

They sat outside at a table in the sun because Jaz said she'd had enough of being cooped up indoors. He pulled his sweater over his head and settled it around her shoulders. A bolt of warmth shot through him when she pulled the sweater around her more securely and huddled down into its warmth. He found himself fighting the urge to warm her up in a far more primitive manner.

'How are you feeling?' he asked when she'd finished her sandwich.

'Actually, as good as new.'

He raised a sceptical eyebrow.

'It's true! I mean, the arm is a bit sore, but other than that…I'm relieved, if the truth be told.'

'Relieved!'

'From the looks on your and Melly's faces, I thought at the very least I was going to need twenty stitches.'

'How many did you get?'

'Three.'

'Three! I thought—'

'You thought I was going to lose my arm.'

He threw his head back and laughed with sheer relief. 'You really are feeling all right?'

'I am.'

'Good. Then I can do this.'

He leaned over and kissed her, savoured all of her sweet goodness with a slowness designed to give as much pleasure as it received. When her lips trembled beneath his, it tested all of his powers of control.

He drew back and touched a finger to her cheek, smiled at the way her breath hitched in her throat. 'I love you, Jaz.'

The words slid out of him as natural as breathing. Then he bent his head and touched his lips to hers again.

CHAPTER ELEVEN

'WHAT on earth…?'

Jaz pushed against him so violently she'd have fallen off her seat if he hadn't grabbed her around the waist to hold her steady.

'What do you think you're doing?' She leapt right out of his arms and stood trembling, facing him.

He'd have laughed out loud at her words if the expression on her face hadn't sliced him to the marrow. 'I thought that was kind of obvious.' He tried to grin that grin—the one that she'd told him eight years ago could make her knees weak. The grin that kicked up one corner of his mouth and said he couldn't think of anything better on this earth than making love with her.

The grin wasn't a lie. He couldn't think of anything he'd rather do.

She stared at his mouth and took a step back, gripped her hands together. 'This can't happen!'

He rose too, planted his feet. He wanted to fill her field of vision the way she filled his. 'Why not?'

'What do you mean, why not? You… I…,' She snapped her mouth shut, dragged in a breath and glared. 'You know why not.'

Her voice trembled. It made him want to smile, to haul her into his arms…to cry.

'Nope, can't say I do.' He shook his head. 'I loved the girl you were eight years ago, and I love the woman you are now even more. I don't get why we can't be together.'

Her eyes grew wide and round. For a brief moment her whole body swayed towards him and a fierce joy gripped him He'd win her round yet. 'There's nothing to stop us from being together, Jaz. Nothing at all.' He'd prove it to her. He took a step towards her, reached out his hands…

Jaz snapped back, away from him. 'I already told you. It's too late!'

Frustration balled through him. And fear. He couldn't lose her a second time. He couldn't.

'When are you going to stop running?'

'Running?' She snorted. 'I'm not running. I came back to Clara Falls, didn't I? And I'm not leaving until my mother's bookshop is back on its feet. Doesn't seem to me that there's much running away involved in any of that.'

At the mention of the bookshop, though, a spasm of pain contracted her nostrils, twisted her mouth. The bookshop. He thought back to the darn loan with its outrageous interest rate that she'd lumbered herself with. He'd have given her the money if she'd let him. He'd have offered to lend it to her, but he'd known she'd have refused that too.

Something told him she would not survive the closure of the bookshop. Financially, she couldn't afford it. Emotionally…a cold chill raised the hairs on the back of his neck.

'Why is the bookshop so important, Jaz?'

Her eyes darkened. Not for the first time, he noticed the circles beneath them. 'Making it a success…it's the only thing left that I can do for my mother.'

It all clicked into place then. He should've realised it right from the start. Her return to Clara Falls; it wasn't about pride or revenge. It wasn't about showing the town she was better than they'd ever given her credit for. It was about love. This woman standing in front of him had only ever been about love.

And yet she held herself responsible for her mother's death. She'd healed all the dark places inside him. He wanted to heal the dark places inside her too. 'When are you going to stop punishing yourself and let yourself be happy?'

'I can't,' she whispered.

The pain in her voice tore at him. 'Why not?' He kept his voice low, but something in her eyes frightened him. He wanted to reach for her but he knew that would only make her retreat further. He clenched his hands and forced them to remain by his sides.

'When you thought I'd cheated on you, it broke my heart, Connor.'

A weight pressed down on his chest, thinning his soul. He deserved her resentment. He sure as hell didn't deserve her forgiveness. And yet he'd thought… 'I've tried to apologise, Jaz. I'm sorrier for that mistake than I can find the words for. If I could turn time back…'

'I know, and it's not what I mean. We both made mistakes we're sorry for. It's…' She broke off to pull his sweater more tightly around her body as if she were cold and couldn't get warm, no matter how hard she tried. 'I became a different person afterwards, that's what I'm trying to tell you. I became bitter and hard, destructive.'

She met his eyes, her own bleak but determined. Bile filled his mouth, his soul.

'I'm not saying I blame you for that because I don't. It wasn't your fault. It was mine. I turned into the kind of person who refused to come back to Clara Falls even though my mother begged me to, even when I knew how much it would mean to her. Can you believe that?'

She gave a harsh laugh. He closed his eyes.

'I may as well have handed my mother that bottle of sleeping pills with my own hands.'

His eyes snapped open. 'You can't believe that!'

Her hands shook. 'But I do.'

'You can't hold yourself responsible for another person's actions like that, Jaz.'

'If I'd come home, I'd have seen how things were. I could've helped. I could've saved her.' She whispered the last sentence.

Then she threw her head back and her eyes blazed. 'But I didn't because I'd turned into some unfeeling monster. That's why there's no future for me and you, Connor. I can't risk loving like that ever again. Who will I hurt or destroy the next time love fails me, huh?'

His mouth had gone dry. 'Who says it will fail?'

She stared back at him—wounded, tired…resolute. 'I'm sorry, Connor, but that's one gamble I'm not prepared to take.'

His stomach…his heart…his whole life, dropped to his feet at the note of finality in her voice. She was wrong, so wrong to exile herself from love like this.

To exile him!

He'd imagined her in his arms so fully and completely, and for all of time. To have her snatched back out of them now was too much to bear. This woman standing in front of him was all about love…but she'd exempted herself. And that meant she'd barred him from love too because he would never settle for second best again. For him, anyone but Jaz Harper was second best.

'According to your philosophy then, I'd better not have the gall to go falling in love again.'

Her jaw dropped, but then she pressed her lips together into a tight line. Pain rolled off her in waves. It took all of his strength not to reach for her and do what he could to wipe that pain away.

'I mean, what if I let jealousy get the better of me again for even half a second? Given my past form, I quite obviously have no right messing with women's hearts.'

She pressed the heels of her hands to her eyes. He hated the defeated slope of her shoulders, the way she seemed unable to throw her head back when she pulled her hands away. 'That's not what I meant and you know it.'

'You said the only thing left that you could do for your mother was to save the bookshop. You're wrong. The best gift you could give Frieda is to live your life fully and without fear…to finally let love back into your life. You don't get it, do you, Jaz? Frieda never wanted you to come back to Clara Falls for her own comfort or peace of mind. She wanted you to come back for yours!'

He watched her try to take in the meaning of his words.

'Do you think she'd be pleased by what you are doing to yourself now?'

She paled.

'Do you think she'd be proud of you?'

She just stared back at him, frozen, and he wondered if he'd pushed her too far. All he wanted to do was drop to his knees in front of her and beg her to be happy.

She took a step away from him. 'Take me home, please, Connor.'

She wouldn't meet his eyes and his heart froze over. 'I'm supposed to be running a book fair. I need to see if I can manage to salvage something from this day.'

And then she turned away and Connor knew that was her final word. His words hadn't breached the walls she had erected around herself.

He'd failed.

They made the fifteen-minute journey from Katoomba hospital to Clara Falls in silence. Jaz's heart hurt with every beat it took, as if someone had taken a baseball bat to it. A pain stretched behind her eyes and into eternity.

The force of Connor's words still pounded at her and she could barely make sense of anything. She'd thought she'd started to put things right, to make things better. Except…

Connor loved her.

One part of her gave a wild, joyful leap. She grabbed it and pulled it back into line. She and Connor?

No.

She forced herself to swallow, to straighten in her seat. They'd reach Clara Falls' main street any moment now.

She realised she still clutched Connor's sweater around her like an offer of comfort. She inhaled one last autumn-scented breath, then folded it neatly and set it on the seat beside her.

She tried to ready herself for the sight of a closed bookshop and no customers, for fairies and pirates who would rightly demand payment anyway. She tried to push to the back of her mind how much money she'd plugged into advertising, on orders for sausages and hiring barbecue plates. She tried to think of ways she could allay the disappointment of the authors and poets who'd promised her their time free of charge this afternoon as a favour to their community.

From the corner of her eye, she saw Connor glance at her. 'You think that Mrs Lavender and co have had to cancel the book fair, don't you?'

She ached to reach out and touch his shoulder, to tell him she'd never meant to hurt him. She didn't. It wouldn't help. 'Yes.'

He frowned. 'Why? Do you think you're that indispensable?'

'Of course not!'

She didn't think she was indispensable to him at all. He'd find someone else to love. One day. And she wanted him to. She gritted her teeth. She meant it. She did. He deserved to be happy.

She reminded herself they were talking about the bookshop. 'Mr Sears will have found a way to sabotage the fair.' And without her there to run the gauntlet...

Her stomach roiled and churned as they turned into Clara Falls' main street.

There weren't as many tourists down this end of the street as usual. Even though the day was disgustingly bright and sunny. Her mouth turned down. She wished for grey skies and hail. Somehow that would make her feel better.

But the sun didn't magically stop shining and rain and huge balls of ice didn't pour down from the sky. She bit back a sigh and kept her eyes doggedly on the streetscape directly beside her.

As they moved closer towards the bookshop, Jaz wanted to close her eyes. She didn't. But she didn't move her eyes past the streetscape directly beside her either. She would not look ahead. She didn't have the heart for that.

She didn't have the heart to glance again at Connor either.

She wished the car would break down. She wished it would come to a clunking halt and just strand her here in the middle of the road, where she wouldn't have to move until it was closing time in Clara Falls.

It didn't happen. The car kept moving forward. Jaz kept her eyes on the view beside her. A few more tourists appeared. At least it wasn't only her shop that was doing poorly today.

Then the scent of frying onions hit her.

Onions!

She slid forward to stare out through the front windscreen.

People.

Oodles and oodles of people. All mingling and laughing out the front of her bookshop.

Connor pulled the car to a halt and a cheer went up when the townsfolk saw her.

A cheer? For her?

Her jaw went slack when she saw who led the cheer.

Mr Sears!

Not only did he lead the cheer but he manned the barbecue hotplate full of sausages too. Carmen grinned and waved from her station beside him. Somehow, Jaz managed to lift her hand and wave back.

Just as many people—perhaps more—were crammed inside the bookshop. It was so full it had almost developed a pulse of its own. She recognised two staff members amid all the chaos, caught sight of a fairy and couldn't help wondering where the pirates had set up for the face painting.

She turned to stare at Connor. 'But what…?'

He didn't smile. He just shrugged. 'Why don't you hop out here? I'll park the car around the back.'

She didn't want to get out of the car. She didn't want to leave him like this. She'd hurt him and…

And she couldn't help him now.

She slid out of the car and stood on the footpath, watched as the car drew away. Only then did she turn back to the crowd and wondered what she should tackle first.

Not what, but who. With a sense of unreality, she made her way through the crowd to Mr Sears. 'I…' She lifted her hands, then let them drop. 'Thank you.' Somehow that seemed completely inadequate.

'No.' He shook his head. 'Thank you.'

And then he smiled. She wondered if she'd ever really seen him smile before.

'In this town, Jaz, we pull together.'

'I… It means a lot.' She found herself smiling back and that didn't seem completely inadequate. It felt right.

She glanced around and what she saw fired hope in her heart. *Oh, Mum, if you could only see this.* She swung back to him. 'What can I do?'

'Carmen and I have things sorted out here for the moment, don't we, Carmen?'

The teenager's eyes danced. 'Aye, aye, Captain.' She saluted her father with the tongs and her sense of fun tugged at Jaz.

He pointed to the door. 'You'll find Audra Lavender and Boyd Longbottom directing proceedings inside.'

She went to turn away, then swung back. 'Did I just hear you say Mrs Lavender *and* Boyd Longbottom?'

'That's right.' He winked. 'I think you'll find it's a day for miracles.'

She started to grin. 'I think you must be right.' She turned and headed for the door.

'Jaz, dear.' Mrs Lavender beamed when she saw her. 'I hope your poor arm is okay.'

'Yes, thank you. It's fine.'

Mrs Lavender had set up two sturdy card tables against the back wall in preparation for the cheese and wine Jaz had ordered for the afternoon readings. She'd pushed the leatherette cubes against the walls and into the spaces between the bookcases. It would leave a circle of space around the authors as they gave their readings. Perfect.

'And the authors can use these tables for signings afterwards, you know, dear. I mean, once the crowd hears our three guests, they're going to want to buy the books. And yes, we do have plenty in stock,' she added when Jaz opened her mouth.

Jaz closed it again, noticed Boyd Longbottom sorting bottles of wine in the stockroom and nodded towards him. 'How?' she whispered.

'I said to him this morning—"Boyd Longbottom, I need help with our Jazmin's book fair and I don't know who else I can ask."'

Jaz's eyes widened. 'It was that easy?'

'Well, now, he did say—"If you agree to have dinner with me tonight then I'm all yours, Audra Lavender." And he said it so nice like. A lady shouldn't turn down a nice offer like that, should she?'

'Of course not.'

Jaz couldn't help thinking back to the way Connor had told her he loved her—as if he couldn't help but say it; as if there hadn't been another thought in his head.

Jaz leant forward and clasped Mrs Lavender's hand. 'I'm pleased for you.'

The older woman's eyes turned misty. 'Thank you, dear. Boyd and I, we've wasted enough time now, I think.'

Jaz straightened and her heart started to thump, but she wasn't sure why. She searched the room for Connor but couldn't see him anywhere. He was the usual reason her heart rate went haywire.

'Mrs Lavender, thank you for everything you've done today. I…'

'Did you really think we'd leave you in the lurch?'

'I certainly didn't expect you to take so much upon yourselves.'

'Why not?'

Jaz stared, and then didn't know quite what to say.

'You've given an old woman a new lease of life. You've

given your staff a fun and harmonious working environment. This book fair, it's galvanised us, made us work together. You've made us feel as if we matter.'

'But you do!'

'Precisely, Jazmin Harper. We all matter. Even you.'

Before Jaz could respond, Mrs Lavender rushed on, 'And I don't know what you did to charm Mr Sears, but it was well done. The moment he saw Boyd and I wrestling with the barbecue, he was across the road like buckshot. He started directing and things just fell into place.'

'I'm very grateful.'

'Jazmin, dear, you're one of us. We look after our own.'

Jaz felt the walls of the community wrap around her and it felt as good as she'd always imagined it would.

'I…well, now that I'm here, what can I do?'

'Mingle. Chat and charm. Bask in the glow of the fair's success. And take care of that arm. Everything else has been taken care of. We know where to find you,' she added when Jaz opened her mouth to argue. 'If we need to.'

Jaz had to content herself with that. She mingled. She chatted. As she moved about the room, it occurred to her that she felt comfortable here—here in Clara Falls, of all places. More comfortable than she had ever felt anywhere in her life before.

'Your mother would've enjoyed this,' Mr Sears said, coming up beside her as the guest authors prepared themselves for the readings.

The scent of frying onions still seasoned the air. She glanced out of the window behind her. Connor had taken over the sausage sizzle. A pulse fluttered in her throat. She had to swallow before she could speak. 'Yes, she would've had a ball.'

Mr Sears followed her gaze. He turned back to her. 'Don't make the same mistakes Frieda and I made.'

'Which was?' She held her breath. It was none of her business but…

He stared back at her. 'I loved your mother from the first

moment I clapped eyes on her.' His lips tightened briefly. 'I understood why she wouldn't get involved with me when I was married. But when my wife died…'

Mrs Sears had died over ten years ago, when Carmen and her brother were just small children.

'I didn't understand why she wouldn't take a chance on us then. I knew she loved me.'

'Didn't she ever tell you why?'

He was quiet for a long moment. 'She said we couldn't be together until all the children were grown up. She said her reputation would make things too difficult for them.'

Jaz's jaw dropped.

'And I took that to mean that she cared more about what people thought than she cared about me.'

He broke off for a moment, then pulled in a breath. 'I wanted the bookshop so badly because I suspected the letters were in the building somewhere. And I wanted it because it was part of her. I treated you very badly, Jazmin. I'm sorry.'

'Apology accepted,' she said without hesitation. 'But, speaking of the bookshop, I am looking for a business partner.'

His eyes suddenly gleamed. 'The two of us could make Frieda's dream a reality.'

She nodded.

'We'll talk about this further.'

She smiled. 'That's what I was hoping you'd say.'

He sobered again. 'I let my disappointment that Frieda wouldn't marry me turn my love into something ugly and twisted.' He reached out, touched her hand briefly. 'Don't you go and make the same mistake.'

Then he was gone.

Jaz's heart pounded and burned. She turned to the partially completed portrait of Frieda on the back wall for guidance. *Oh, Mum, what do I do?*

The partially completed portrait didn't give her so much as a hint or clue.

Perhaps if Jaz could finish it…but she couldn't seem to bear to.

It wasn't that she couldn't bear to. She simply couldn't do it—it was as plain as that. Something blocked her, something stood between her and her ability to find and execute that final essence of Frieda.

Would Frieda want her to take a chance on Connor?

She glanced out of the window again. Sun glinted off his hair and yearning gripped her. But…

No! Fear filled her soul. She couldn't risk it; she just couldn't. She'd won more today than she had ever expected. She had to content herself with that. It would have to do.

The rest of the afternoon breezed along without so much as the tiniest push from Jaz. Everyone agreed that the author readings were a huge hit—not least the authors, who must've sold dozens of their books between them.

Connor packed up the sausage sizzle and disappeared. Jaz did her best not to notice.

Just when she thought the day was starting to wind down, a new buzz started up. Connor stood at the back of the room, in the same spot the guest authors had, calling for everyone's attention.

Jaz blinked and straightened. She chafed her arms and tried to look nonchalant.

'As most of you know, today wouldn't have been possible if it wasn't for one special lady—Jaz Harper.'

She gulped, tried to smile at the applause that broke out around her.

'Jaz returned to Clara Falls to honour her mother's memory, and to make her mother's final dream a reality. I can't tell you all how glad I am to see the town come out in such numbers to support her.'

Jaz noticed then that most of the tourists had wandered off—they'd probably left after the readings. The people who were left were almost all locals.

Connor gestured to the partially completed portrait on the

wall behind him. 'As you can see, Jaz means to leave a lasting memorial of her mother here in Clara Falls. It only seems fitting that the grand finale to the day should be Jaz putting the finishing touches to her mother's portrait. If you agree, put your hands together and we'll get her up here to do exactly that.'

No way! He couldn't force her hand this way. She wouldn't do it. She *couldn't* do it.

But a path had opened up between her and Connor and everyone was clapping. Some people cheered, yet others stomped their feet, and Jaz had no choice but to move forward.

'What is this?' she hissed when she reached him. 'Payback?'

'Just finish the damn picture, Jaz.'

His voice was hard, unrelenting, but when she glanced into his face the gold highlights in his eyes gleamed out at her. 'Connor, I can't.' She was ashamed at the way her voice wobbled, but she couldn't help it.

He took her hands in his. 'What is it you focus on in the photographs that you turn into tattoos? What is it that you see in those photographs of people you don't know, but capture so completely that you bring tears to the eyes of their loved ones?'

She searched his eyes. 'Details,' she finally whispered. She focused on the details—one thing at a time, utterly and completely.

'Will you trust me on this?'

She stared at him for a long moment, then nodded. 'Yes.'

He wouldn't lead her astray on something so important. Even though she had hurt him. She knew that with her whole heart. He would try to help her the way she'd helped him.

He handed her the photograph of her mother. 'Forget that she's your mother, forget that you ever knew her, and focus only on the details.'

She stared at the photograph. The details. Right.

Then he handed her a paintbrush. 'Paint, Jaz.' Only then did she notice that he'd already arranged her paints about her.

Jaz painted. The scent of autumn engulfed her and she painted.

She'd finished the eyes and nose, the brow and the wild hair already. Now she focused on the mouth—the lips wide open in laughter, creases and laughter lines fanning out from the corners. She focused on the strong, square jaw with its beauty spot, then the neck and the shoulders.

She lost herself in details.

As always happened, when Jaz finished the last stroke she had no idea how much time had passed. She set her paintbrush down and stepped back, and the room gave a collective gasp. Jaz heard it for what it was—awe. It meant she'd done a good job.

She couldn't look yet. She needed all those details to fade from her mind first.

She pressed the heels of her hands to her eyes, unutterably weary. Strong arms went around her and drew her in close, soaking her in their warmth and strength. She wanted to shelter in those arms—Connor's arms—for ever. He'd remained standing behind her the entire time she'd painted, his presence urging her on, ordering her to stay focused. And she had.

But she couldn't stay here in his arms. At least, not for ever. She'd already made that decision—she couldn't afford to let the worst of her nature free in the world again.

But, before she was ready to let him go, he was putting her from him. 'Are you ready to see it?'

She pulled in a shaky breath, managed a nod. He eased her back towards the crowd, then slowly turned her around to face her finished artwork.

Jaz stared. And then she staggered as the impact of the portrait hit her. She'd have fallen flat on her face if Connor hadn't kept an arm around her.

Frieda laughing in the sun.

Her mother stood in front of her laughing, filled with happiness and goodwill and her own unique brand of fun, and Jaz ached to reach out and touch her. *This* was how Frieda would want Jaz to remember her. *This* was how Frieda would want everyone to remember her.

Oh, Mum, I loved you. You did know that, didn't you?

Yes. The word drifted to her on an autumn-scented breeze and suddenly her cheeks were wet with all the tears she hadn't yet shed. The tightness in her chest started to ease.

Oh, Mum, what do I do?

No answer came back to her on a breeze—autumn-scented or otherwise, but the answer started to grow in Jaz's heart the longer she stared at Frieda's portrait.

Be happy. That was what her mother would say. It was all that Frieda had ever wanted for her.

Did she dare?

She scrubbed the tears from her cheeks with hands that shook, then turned to face the hushed crowd that stood at her back. 'I want to thank you all for coming here today—for supporting me and Frieda and the bookshop. If she could, I know my mother would thank you too.' She paused, dragged in a breath. 'I came back to Clara Falls with a grudge in my heart, but it's gone now. I've finally realised my true home is here in Clara Falls and—' she found herself smiling '—it's good to be back.'

The crowd broke into a loud round of applause. Mr Sears brought it back under control after what seemed like an age. 'Okay, folks, that's officially the end to the book fair…' he sent Jaz a sly look '…for this year, at least.'

Good Lord!

She thought about it. An annual event? The idea had merit.

'Now, there's still plenty of cleaning up to be done,' Mr Sears continued, 'so those of you who are willing to stick around…'

Jaz couldn't help but grin as he took control.

Connor touched her arm. 'Jaz. I… It's time I headed off.'

The golden lights in his eyes had disappeared. Leaving? But…no! She didn't want him to go.

Her mouth went dry. *She didn't want him to go.* It hit her then. Denying herself the chance of building a life with Connor, of being with him—that was hurting her just as much as his lack of faith in her had eight years ago.

Did that mean she'd turn back into that desperate, destructive person she feared so much?

She all but stopped breathing. Her fingernails bit into her palms. She hunched into herself and waited for the blackness, the anger, to engulf her again…and kept waiting.

She lifted her head a little, dragged in a shaky breath, and counted to three. She lifted her head a little higher, and slowly it dawned on her. The blackness—it wasn't coming back.

She'd learned from the mistakes of the past.

She was stronger, older, wiser.

She wasn't afraid any more!

She wanted to dance. To sing and dance and—

She glanced into Connor's face and the singing and dancing inside her abruptly stopped. Had she left it too late? Had Connor finally run out of patience…and love?

She glanced at Frieda's portrait, then back at Connor.

'I love you.' She said the words as simply and plainly as he had to her earlier in the day. She didn't know if it was too late to say them or not. She only knew she had to say them.

Connor froze. He backed up a step. 'What did you just say?'

She grew aware that the people nearest to them had turned to stare. She leaned in close to him and whispered the words again. 'I love you, Connor.'

He threw his head back, his eyes blazed. 'Are you ashamed of your feelings or something?'

'No, I'm not ashamed that I love you, Connor.' She said the words, loud and proud. 'It's just that guys aren't as gushy-gushy as girls and I thought you might like to have this conversation in private, that's all.'

He just stared at her. He didn't move. He didn't say anything. He had to have heard her. She'd said it three times!

'It's customary for the boy to kiss the girl at this point,' Mrs Lavender pointed out. 'And if that is your intention, Connor Reed, then I definitely suggest you find yourself some privacy.'

Her words acted on him like magic. He grabbed Jaz's hand,

pulled her through the stockroom, out through the kitchenette and all the way outside. He dropped her hand again and swung around to stare at her.

'You're not kissing me yet,' Jaz couldn't help but point out.

'Not yet.' He pointed a finger at her. It shook. 'You say that you love me.'

'Yes.'

'Why the change of heart?'

'It's not really a change of heart. I've always loved you.' The way she sensed he'd always loved her.

'What made you change your mind about taking the risk?'

'Frieda.' She said her mother's name simply. 'I couldn't finish her portrait because I was blocked. I was blocked because you were right. I wasn't living my life the way she'd have wanted. When I looked at the finished portrait I finally realised what she'd want me to do.'

He frowned. 'To tell me you love me?'

'To be happy,' she corrected softly. 'And being with you is what makes me the happiest.'

His eyes darkened with intent then. Her pulse leapt. He moved towards her . .

It started to rain.

'I don't believe this,' Jaz murmured under her breath. 'Not now!'

She glanced from the sky with its lowering clouds to Connor. 'We could…er…always go up to my flat.'

The gold highlights in his eyes glittered. He reached out and captured her chin in his strong callused fingers. 'If you invite me up there, Jaz, I won't be leaving any time soon.'

A thrill shot through her. The rain continued to fall around them. 'Where's Melly?' she managed.

'With my parents. My father is going to drop her off at Yvonne's party tonight.'

Jaz stared up at the rain again, then back at Connor. 'So you don't have anywhere you need to be tonight?'

'No.'

'Then…'

'Then…?' he mimicked.

Jaz groaned. 'Kiss me, Connor.'

He did.

When he lifted his head, long moments later, she could hardly breathe let alone stand. 'Come on.' When the strength returned to her limbs, she grabbed his hand and headed up the stairs and to her flat.

Connor took the keys from her fingers and turned her to face him, heedless of the rain. 'I'm not prepared to lose you a second time, Jaz. I want you to know that this—' he nodded at the door '—is for keeps. I need to know that you feel the same way.'

Her heart expanded until she thought it might burst. 'For keeps,' she whispered. She'd never been surer of anything in her life. It made a mockery of all her previous doubts.

'For ever?' he demanded.

'And ever,' she agreed.

He rested his forehead against hers. 'I love you with all that's in me, Jaz Harper. Promise me you will never run away again. I don't think I could bear it.'

His eyes darkened with remembered pain. She reached up and brushed his hair from his forehead. 'I promise.' Then she kissed him with all the love in her heart.

They were both breathing hard when she drew back.

'In return,' he rasped, holding her gaze, 'I swear to you that I will always listen to you. I won't jump to stupid conclusions.'

'I know,' she said. But it suddenly occurred to her that, even if he did, they were both stronger now. Together, they could overcome anything.

She didn't know why, but she found herself suddenly laughing in his arms, so glad to be near him and loving him, revelling in the freedom of it.

'What do you young people think you're doing up there?' Mrs Lavender called from below, her voice tart with outrage.

'Don't you know it's raining? Get inside with you before you catch your deaths!'

'Better do what the lady says,' Connor said with a lazy grin, unlocking the door.

Jaz's heart leapt. 'Absolutely,' she agreed, the breath catching in her throat.

He held his hand out to her. She placed hers in it. Together they stepped over the threshold.

HARLEQUIN
60 YEARS
of pure reading pleasure

We'll be spotlighting a different series
every month throughout 2009
to celebrate our 60th anniversary.

**Look for Harlequin® Superromance®
in September!**

THE
DIAMOND
Legacy

*Celebrate with
The Diamond Legacy
miniseries!*

Follow the stories of four cousins as they come to terms
with the complications of love and what it means to
be a family. Discover with them the sixty-year-old secret
that rocks not one but two families.

A DAUGHTER'S TRUST by *Tara Taylor Quinn*
September

FOR THE LOVE OF FAMILY by *Kathleen O'Brien*
October

LIKE FATHER, LIKE SON by *Karina Bliss*
November

A MOTHER'S SECRET by *Janice Kay Johnson*
December

Available wherever books are sold.

REQUEST YOUR FREE BOOKS!
2 FREE NOVELS PLUS 2
FREE GIFTS!

HARLEQUIN® *Romance*®

From the Heart, For the Heart

YES! Please send me 2 FREE Harlequin® Romance novels and my 2 FREE gifts (gifts are worth about $10). After receiving them, if I don't wish to receive any more books, I can return the shipping statement marked "cancel". If I don't cancel, I will receive 4 brand-new novels every month and be billed just $3.84 per book in the U.S. or $4.24 per book in Canada. That's a savings of at least 15% off the cover price! It's quite a bargain! Shipping and handling is just 50¢ per book.* I understand that accepting the 2 free books and gifts places me under no obligation to buy anything. I can always return a shipment and cancel at any time. Even if I never buy another book, the two free books and gifts are mine to keep forever.

114 HDN EYU3   314 HDN EYKG

Name	(PLEASE PRINT)

Address	Apt. #

City	State/Prov.	Zip/Postal Code

Signature (if under 18, a parent or guardian must sign)

Mail to the **Harlequin Reader Service:**
IN U.S.A.: P.O. Box 1867, Buffalo, NY 14240-1867
IN CANADA: P.O. Box 609, Fort Erie, Ontario L2A 5X3

Not valid to current subscribers of Harlequin Romance books.

**Are you a subscriber of Harlequin Romance books
and want to receive the larger-print edition?
Call 1-800-873-8635 today!**

* Terms and prices subject to change without notice. Prices do not include applicable taxes. Sales tax applicable in N.Y. Canadian residents will be charged applicable provincial taxes and GST. Offer not valid in Quebec. This offer is limited to one order per household. All orders subject to approval. Credit or debit balances in a customer's account(s) may be offset by any other outstanding balance owed by or to the customer. Please allow 4 to 6 weeks for delivery. Offer available while quantities last.

Your Privacy: Harlequin Books is committed to protecting your privacy. Our Privacy Policy is available online at www.eHarlequin.com or upon request from the Reader Service. From time to time we make our lists of customers available to reputable third parties who may have a product or service of interest to you. If you would prefer we not share your name and address, please check here. ☐

HR09R

HARLEQUIN Romance

Coming Next Month

Available September 8, 2009

This fall, curl up and relax with a Harlequin Romance® novel!

#4117 KEEPING HER BABY'S SECRET Raye Morgan
Baby on Board
Cameron's from the richest family in town. Diana's pregnant, unwed and definitely unsuitable. But will it stop these old friends from falling in love?

#4118 CLAIMED: SECRET ROYAL SON Marion Lennox
Marrying His Majesty
A year ago, Lily accidentally became pregnant with Prince Alexandros's baby. Now Alex wants to claim his son. Will Lily agree to *Marrying His Majesty?* Find out in the first book of this new trilogy!

#4119 EXPECTING MIRACLE TWINS Barbara Hannay
Follow surrogate mom Mattie's *Baby Steps to Marriage...*in the first of a new duet by Barbara Hannay. How can Mattie begin a relationship with gorgeous Jake when she's expecting twin trouble?

#4120 MEMO: THE BILLIONAIRE'S PROPOSAL Melissa McClone
9 to 5
When Chaney finds herself back working with billionaire playboy Drake, she must remember how he broke her heart, *not* his devastating charm... Oops!

#4121 A TRIP WITH THE TYCOON Nicola Marsh
Escape Around the World
Join Tamara as she travels through India on a trip of a lifetime, and catch the fireworks when she bumps into a blast from her past, maverick entrepreneur Ethan.

#4122 INVITATION TO THE BOSS'S BALL Fiona Harper
In Her Shoes...
Watch in wonder as this plain Jane is transformed from pumpkin to princess when she's hired to organize her boss's company ball...and dance in his oh-so-delicious arms!

HRCNMBPA0809